CRAZY FOR YOU

Abby Farnsworth

World Castle Publishing, LLC
Pensacola, Florida

Hardback ISBN: 9798248800995
Paperback ISBN: 9798891265301
eBook ISBN: 9798891265318
First Edition World Castle Publishing, LLC, April 6, 2026
http://www.worldcastlepublishing.com

Licensing Notes

Cover: Cover Designs by Karen
Editor: Karen Fuller

Dedication:

To all the girls who wished that Catherine would have chosen Heathcliff in Wuthering Heights, this is for you.

Author's Note:

Dear Reader,

Whether you're new here or have stuck around for a while, welcome! This is my first adult romance, and I'm super excited to share it with you. Cain and Brea are one of my favorite couples I've ever written. If you love anti-heroes, Cain is going to be your guy. He is Heathcliff, Christian Grey, and so many others wrapped into one handsome package, but without any adult content. Please enjoy and dream about finding a brooding billionaire of your own.

Happy reading and good luck out there,
Abby

Acknowledgments:

Of course, thank you to Karen Fuller and World Castle Publishing! Thanks to my family, friends, and everyone else who has and continues to support me. You guys are the best. Of course, thank you to Scott and Zeus, my two favorite guys. I love you both. And thank you to my wonderful readers, especially those who stay with me through genre changes and all the ups and downs that come with being a creative. Your kind words and reviews mean the world. Hang in there and hold on for happy endings.

Chapter One

CALM BEFORE THE STORM

Brea

Mila stared at me from across the room, her bright blue eyes glimmering with a hint of mischief. I shook my head, trying to convince her not to do whatever she had in mind. Mila had always been the adventurous type. We'd been best friends since middle school, when she had decided to pull me into her (now our) friend group; I still had no idea what inspired her to do so. But seventh grade had been almost a decade ago, and now we were adults, at least theoretically.

Mila, with her long blond curls falling down to her waist and wearing a tiny black dress, crept up behind our mutual friend, Evan. I frowned, which only made her smile grow. While Evan was busy texting, Mila slowly reached out to grab his Sprite, swapping it with a simple glass of ice water. Evan was blissfully unaware of her actions, but when he reached down and took another sip of his drink, he almost spit it out.

"Really, Mila?" Evan said. "Hilarious."

She smiled at him. "Just keeping you on your

toes."

If I hadn't known Evan for years, I might have thought the expression on his face was one of annoyance. But the truth was, he adored her attention. While Mila still refused to accept the truth, Evan was desperately in love with her. He had been since we were all kids. But between seventh grade and the summer before our sophomore year of college, not much had changed. He still looked at her like a star-struck schoolboy. Despite my constant hints, she still didn't view him as anything more than a brother. Honestly, I would have loved for them to end up together, but I didn't see that happening anytime soon.

Evan and his twin brother, Enzo, were unquestionably my two best friends, apart from Mila. Like me, Evan and Enzo had always been shy and more than a little bit nerdy. Mila was the exact opposite. She seemed to collect introverts wherever she went and add them to her pack. It had paid off, at least during school, since she probably wouldn't have made it through Algebra without Evan's...assistance. Now, we were just a group of old friends who still managed to find the time to hang out during summer breaks.

"Hey Evan, come check out this girl that just messaged me," Enzo said.

Mila made it to Enzo's side before Evan had taken a step in that direction.

"Let me see," Mila said.

Enzo handed her his phone. "She's cute, right? And she's a barista. What could be better? You know I love brunettes."

Mila shrugged. "She needs a new wardrobe, but that can be resolved. Bring her around sometime, and I can make her sparkle like a diamond straight from the jeweler."

"I don't think I should tell her that," Enzo said, frowning.

Mila rolled her eyes. "No, Enzo, obviously not."

Evan looked away, rolling his eyes. I gave him a sympathetic smile. Although Evan had never actually told me about his feelings for Mila, we had a sort of unspoken understanding.

"Brea, you start your new job tomorrow, right?" Mila asked.

"Bright and early," I replied.

Evan pursed his lips. "Remember what I said about Cain, Brea. He can be a real pain. If he's too hard on you, just let me know. I'll talk to him."

My new boss for the summer, Cain Kingston, was Evan and Enzo's cousin. They were the reason I got the internship in the first place. I never should have been made personal assistant to the CEO of a luxury jewelry brand before my sophomore year of college, but when Evan and Enzo offered me the job, I couldn't say no. After all, their father was the founder. Evan had originally been intended to take over the company after his father retired, but he and Enzo were far more interested in philanthropy than money-making. Lucky for them, they had enough of a fortune to spend their lives throwing as many charity functions as they wanted without ever worrying about supporting themselves. Mila was from a similar situation. She was the only daughter of a well-respected fashion designer. Scholarships were the only reason I had ever been able to attend the same private school as the three of them. But they had never made me feel left out or lesser because we were in different tax brackets.

"I don't know why you two would have even set Brea up for the job when you know Cain is going to be mean to her," Mila said.

"Because it pays more than she ever would have made working a normal summer job," Evan said, "and you know as well as I do that Brea would never take money from us."

I rolled my eyes. "I don't need charity, guys."

Enzo rolled his eyes. "Don't be so dramatic, Brea. We just want you to be able to retire while you still have breath in your lungs. Early childhood education isn't known for its high-paying salaries."

That was the truth. None of my friends supported my dream of owning and operating a preschool for disadvantaged children. Well, at least not under my terms. Evan and Enzo had both offered me lump sums of money to establish my school, using the excuse that they could write the donation off on their taxes. I didn't want to take money from my friends, though. It would drastically change our relationships.

"Andddd she won't just let us give her the money," Evan added.

"Ugh, come on, Brea," Mila said. "If you just accept the loan, we could spend the summer sunbathing instead and getting a nice tan. And I don't want to go bikini shopping by myself."

I shook my head. "Nope, I'm doing this on my own. And you can't exactly call it a loan when all of you refuse to let me pay interest."

"That is an entirely irrelevant detail," Mila said, rolling her eyes.

I rolled my shoulder, accidentally letting out a long yawn.

"Oh no," Evan said, "someone's tired."

"You'd better get home and go to sleep," Enzo added.

"You could just crash here," Mila interjected. "The guest room is always open to you. We could have a sleepover."

I shook my head. "Nope, I need to get some real sleep tonight. Whenever I stay here, I never end up going to bed until after midnight. I need energy for tomorrow, especially if Cain is as much of a nightmare as Evan says."

"Oh, trust me," Enzo replied, "he is. I could

never work for him."

I grabbed my purse off the kitchen island, walking to the door of Mila's apartment. "Don't worry, I won't give up so easily."

"Goodnight, Brea!" Mila called.

"Goodnight," I responded, closing the door behind me.

Chapter Two

RED

Brea

I stared at myself in the mirror, gently running my fingers through my cocoa-colored hair to give the curls a more relaxed look. Even though I was typically confident, or at least content, with my appearance, I was still nervous since it was my first day on the job. There really wasn't any need to be concerned, though. My eyeliner was perfectly applied, and my natural lashes were long enough that they only required a little mascara to make them look full and defined. The black pencil skirt and sky-blue blouse I had selected was one of my favorite outfit combinations, so it seemed like the ideal choice for such an important day. To give the look an elegant finish, I decided to wear a pair of black kitten heels. I felt both professional and confident, which was just what I needed.

After driving the fifteen-minute commute to the Kingston Headquarters, I gave myself a few moments to sit and admire the building. I had visited the monstrosity of an office building before, but the dark, gothic architecture looked far more intimidating now that I was officially an employee. After taking a deep breath, I stepped out of my car, grabbed my briefcase, and headed inside. As my heels clicked against the concrete, I gathered my confidence and mentally prepared to meet my slightly terrifying new boss.

After entering the building, I walked straight toward the elevator and hit the button for the tenth floor. The only person in the lobby was a receptionist sitting behind a desk, and she didn't even look my way. It was just a few moments until I heard a chime, and then watched as the doors opened. As soon as the elevator stopped moving and I stepped out, I was immediately blown away. Although I had visited the lower levels before, I had never been allowed access to the top floor, where Cain's office was located. While the entire building was beautiful, this was a whole other world. The floors of the flawless black marble and the walls were painted a deep, luxurious crimson. Hanging from the ceiling was a startling silver chandelier that illuminated the entire space with a soft glow. The overwhelming display of wealth certainly didn't help calm my nerves.

"Can I help you?" A sweet voice asked.

Directly in front of me was a beautiful woman, likely only a few years older than me. She sat at an executive-style desk with nothing other than a large desktop computer in front of her.

"Oh, yes. I'm Mr. Kingston's new personal assistant. I wasn't given any directions other than to come to the tenth floor," I replied.

She smiled at me. "Brea, it's so nice to meet you. I'm Olive, Mr. Kingston's secretary. I answer emails and do all of the other boring stuff. If you ever need help with anything, you can just let me know. I'm sort of like the oil that keeps this crazy machine running."

"It's nice to meet you, too," I said. "Do you know where I should go?"

Olive nodded, pointing toward a set of large double doors. "His office is just through there. It's unlocked, but I always knock before going inside. Sometimes it's best not to enter when he's…in a particular mood."

I raised my eyebrows. "What does that mean?"

She bit her lip. "You'll understand soon."

"Should I be concerned?" I asked.

"Oh, no. You'll be fine. Just try not to upset him," she replied.

I nodded. "Right, I'll do my best.

"Good luck!" she replied.

"Thanks."

As I approached the double doors, I attempted to stop my hands from shaking. The fact that Cain had a temper certainly wasn't a surprise to me. Still, I hadn't known that it was so bad that his secretary would warn me about it right off the bat. Maybe this whole thing was a mistake, I wondered. I shook my head, no, you can't let yourself think like that. Taking a deep breath, I raised my right hand to knock on the door.

I jumped a bit when a deep, booming voice replied. "Come in."

The handle clicked as I opened the door and stepped into Cain's office. Once again, I was stunned speechless. This room was even more shocking than the last. From floor to ceiling, every surface was black. The only light came from red LED lights that lined the walls. I felt goosebumps begin to pop up on my arms. There were just a few pieces of furniture in the room: a large, leather couch, and a desk with an armchair behind it.

The most breathtaking thing of all, though, was the man who stood in front of me. I had seen pictures of Cain before, but none of them did him justice. He was, without a doubt, the most gorgeous man I'd ever seen. With silky black hair, olive-toned skin, and piercing blue eyes, Cain looked like he'd just stepped out of a painting. He wore black pants with a half-unbuttoned white shirt. Even leaning back against his desk, Cain still towered over me. It took a few moments before I finally realized I was holding my breath.

"Ms. Paige," he said, "welcome to Kingston Headquarters."

I blinked a few times, trying to clear my mind.

"Thank you, sir. I'm happy to be here."

He nodded. "Good."

A few moments of silence passed as Cain simply stared at me. I looked down at the floor, waiting for him to speak. With each breath, I grew more and more anxious. His gaze felt like fire blazing across my skin. The man radiated dominance.

"What are you wearing?" he asked.

I looked up in confusion. "Just…clothes."

He shook his head. "You'll need to change."

I began to panic. "Is there something wrong with what I'm wearing? I wasn't given any guidelines or information about a uniform."

He rolled his eyes. "I should have known my cousins wouldn't tell you anything. You'll need to wear a red dress."

"Today?" I asked.

"No," he replied, "every day."

I attempted to hide the confusion in my voice. "Um, why?"

His eyes met mine, annoyance beginning to show. "Because it's what I want."

I bit my lip. "I don't have any red dresses."

"That's fine," he replied, "I'll send Olive to go get some for you."

He turned and walked to sit behind his desk.

"Mr. Kingston, I don't really have a lot of extra funds to spend at the moment. That's kind of why I'm working a summer job."

He almost laughed. "That's fine, Brea. I wasn't expecting you to pay for them. Olive has access to my personal account; she'll use my card."

My eyes grew wide. "Oh, uh, thank you."

"Don't worry about it," he replied, "anything you need for this position, I'll cover." Cain reached into his desk and pulled out a manila envelope. He motioned for me to sit on the couch facing him. "Please, sit."

I sat on the couch, placing my briefcase on the floor beside me. Cain handed me the envelope. I took it from him, unsure if I was supposed to open it. For some reason, I couldn't seem to function properly around him.

"Inside you'll find your advance, as well as some paperwork you'll need to sign. Most of it is typical, apart from the NDA," he said.

I raised my eyebrows. "NDA?"

"Nondisclosure agreement," Cain replied.

"I know what it is, but why do I have to sign one?" I asked.

He leaned forward, resting his elbows on the desk. "You're the personal assistant to a billionaire, Brea. All of my staff are required to sign one."

"Everyone in this building has signed an NDA?" I replied, shocked.

He shook his head. "No, just everyone who

lives in my home."

My jaw dropped. "Excuse me?"

"They didn't tell you that either?" Cain asked, his voice full of frustration .

I shook my head. "No."

"Well, don't worry, it's only temporary. Of course, you'll have your own bedroom, bathroom, and living area. After you vacate the position in August, you can move back to your apartment," he replied.

"But...I haven't agreed to live with you yet. What about all my things and my apartment? I can't just pick up and move with no warning," I said.

Cain tilted his head to the side. "Do you want the job, Brea?"

I nodded, anxiety coursing through me. "Yes."

"Then you've agreed," he replied.

I sat perfectly still, utterly speechless. The entire situation was completely absurd. I'd had jobs before, but none like this. Moments later, the door opened. A man wearing a black suit stepped inside. His face was completely expressionless.

"Brea, meet Wolf. He's my bodyguard and driver. He'll take you back to my home now. We're done for today," Cain said.

I looked between the two men. "What?"

Cain nodded. "As you didn't bring anything with you, I'll have all the personal items you might need for the next few months delivered to the house. Just look over the paperwork and prepare for tomorrow. It'll be a busy day."

Wolf opened the door and motioned for me to follow him. "Please come with me, Ms. Paige."

Having no other choice, I took one last look at Cain before following Wolf away from one of the strangest experiences of my life. *Focus on the money, Brea,* I thought to myself. *That's all that matters.*

Chapter Three

THE MANSION

Brea

Wolf didn't speak a single word during the drive to Cain's house. When we pulled into the driveway, I couldn't help but stare out the window in awe. The house was constructed out of dark stone with dozens of windows, and was surrounded by sprawling green gardens that seemed to stretch on forever. I couldn't imagine why a single man would need such a large home. Then again, I had no idea how many members of Cain's staff lived with him.

Wolf parked the car right in front of the house. I stood silently as he unlocked the front door. He stepped aside, motioning for me to walk in ahead of him. The entryway was exactly what I had expected after seeing Cain's office. The floor was a dark hardwood, and all the walls were, unsurprisingly, painted black. A chandelier, much larger than the one on the 10th floor of the Kingston building, hung from the ceiling. There was no artwork or decorations anywhere, which made sense. Cain didn't really seem like the decorating type.

Before me was a large double staircase that led in two opposite directions.

After locking the front door behind him, Wolf moved past me and began walking up the stairs. Not knowing what else to do, I followed him. He was a quick walker, so it took me a moment to catch up.

"Um, excuse me," I said.

Wolf turned around. "Yes?"

I pointed in the opposite direction from where we were going. "What's that way? This place is huge, and if I'm going to be staying here, I'd like to know my way around."

"That leads to the offices and staff residences," Wolf replied.

"Shouldn't we be going there , then?" I asked.

Wolf shook his head. "No, you and I are the only ones with rooms near Mr. Kingston's."

He began walking again, and I followed along. "Why? I mean, I understand why you need to be close. But what about me? Why am I even staying here, anyway? And how many people live in this house?"

Wolf paused his walking again. "You ask a lot of questions. All I know is that Mr. Kingston likes his personal assistant to be close. Remember, you work directly for him, not the company. There is a variety of staff here. Apart from you and me, there's also a cook, a housekeeper, a gardener, and a manager."

"Just one more question," I said. "What does a

manager do?"

"She makes sure everything runs smoothly, keeps an inventory of household items, and organizes any events that Mr. Kingston may want to host," he replied. "Now, no more questions."

Wolf continued walking up the stairs, and I followed him in silence. I still had about two dozen more things I'd like to ask, but he didn't seem like the talkative type. When I called Evan and Enzo, we were going to have a serious discussion about sharing important information with each other. Wolf led me down a long hallway with a variety of closed doors that I assumed were not intended for me to open, so I did my best to prevent my curiosity from causing any more problems than it already had. He stopped at the very end of the hallway, where a window and one last door were located.

"This is your room," he replied.

"No key?" I asked.

He shook his head. "You can lock it from the inside when you're in there. Apart from that, you don't need to worry about it being unlocked. We don't have a theft problem in this house."

"Right," I replied. "Makes sense."

Wolf stood silently, seemingly waiting for me to go inside. After deciding I wasn't going to get any more information out of him, I opened the door. A moment later, Wolf was already halfway back down the hallway.

I stepped inside what was apparently going to be my new home for the next few months. Although I could acknowledge how crazy all of this was, the fact that I had actually agreed to it hadn't registered with me yet. But the room was beautiful.

I closed the door behind me, amazed at the stark contrast between my new living space and the rest of Cain's house. Everything was so open and bright. On the far side of the room was a huge window with a built-in bench. It provided a stunning view of the luscious gardens that were teeming with life. Against the back wall was a huge, king-size four-poster canopy bed. With light, soft, pastel pink blankets and probably a dozen fluffy pillows, it looked like the most comfortable place in the world. The floor was a pale wood, maybe bamboo, but it was mostly covered by an off-white area rug that matched the color of the walls. Across from the bed was a gas fireplace that looked to be more for decoration than anything else. But the best part of all was that there were books everywhere. Bookshelves lined the walls, barely leaving enough space to actually tell what color they were. I stared in amazement, admiring the amount of color they brought to the room.

There were three doors inside the bedroom, one of which led to a large, walk-in closet. The fact that I hadn't brought anything to sleep in certainly didn't seem to be a problem. A whole section of the closet was dedicated to pajamas. There was another for loungewear, one for athletic clothes, and then a whole wall for what was probably fifty different red dresses. How on earth Cain had managed to have them delivered so quickly was a mystery. And what was even more shocking was that everything seemed to be in my size. In the center of the room was an island of sorts that held a variety of shoes and purses. I could barely believe the amount of money he'd invested just in the contents of the closet alone.

The next door opened into the nicest bathroom I had ever seen. The floors were a smooth, white marble that flowed directly into a rainwater-style shower that covered the entire back wall. Beside the shower was a clawfoot tub that was large enough to give a horse a bath, and there was, of course, a toilet and sink. On the other side of the room, facing another large window, was a vanity filled with every product imaginable. It was stocked with luxury perfumes, designer makeup, and every hair product anyone could ever need.

The final door led to a living area with two velvet couches, a coffee table, and a desk. After everything I'd discovered so far, I wasn't surprised to find a new laptop with a note from Cain waiting for me.

Ms. Paige,

I hope you're satisfied with the

space provided for you. If you find it too objectionable, you're free to change it as you see fit. However, my housekeeper, Ms. Ramirez, did put a good deal of effort into curating the space, so she might be a bit offended if you make too many changes. Please look over the paperwork.

I'll see you soon,
Kingston

I ran my fingers over the letter, admiring Cain's handwriting. It was brief, but not…cold. To be honest, I wasn't exactly sure what to make of all this. Cain was certainly a mystery.

I sat down on the closest couch and opened the manila envelope. Until reading the letter, I'd almost forgotten about the paperwork, including the NDA. Everything was happening so quickly that I could barely keep track. It made sense that a billionaire would want to keep his personal life private. But if he was so concerned about maintaining that, then why did he have me, a girl he'd never met before, move into his side of the house when there was a whole other staff residential area? Apart from Evan and Enzo's words, he had no reason to believe I was trustworthy. I had a feeling that even after I signed my name on the dotted line, I still wouldn't fully understand exactly what was going on.

The first papers I pulled out of the envelope were pretty standard. He wanted all the normal information. I filled them out without a second thought. Afterall, he was paying me well. But when I came across the small slip of paper with five thousand dollars written on it as my advance, I gasped out loud. I knew that for a billionaire, signing a check for that amount of money wasn't a big deal. But for me, a college student, it was huge. Why would he give me such a big bonus, especially when he had no idea if I would do my job successfully? Was the service I would be providing even worth that amount?

Moments later, I heard a knock on the bedroom door. I rushed over to open it, wondering if perhaps Cain had changed his mind and found something for me to do. But when I opened the door, I was met with the face of a middle-aged woman with a kind smile and large, curious eyes. She had light brown skin and was wearing a pair of khaki pants and a practical, black button-up shirt. I ran through the possibilities in my mind, trying to determine which member of staff she might be.

"Ms. Paige?" she asked.

I nodded. "Yes, but please just call me Brea."

"It's so nice to meet you. I'm Bianca, Mr. Kingston's housekeeper," she replied. "Do you like your rooms?"

"Oh, they're perfect! Not at all what I was

expecting given Mr. Kingston's typical taste," I answered.

She smiled. "Well, all I was told is that your favorite color is pink and that you enjoy reading. I tried my best with that limited information."

I attempted to prevent her from hearing the confusion in my voice. "You mean, you moved all these books in here for me?"

"Of course," she replied. "Mr. Kingston said to make sure you were as comfortable as possible. I thought that if you enjoyed reading, being surrounded by books might make you feel more at home."

It took a few moments before I was able to reply. "Thank you for being so thoughtful."

"Of course," she said. "Oh, and I'll bring you dinner up at 6 o'clock."

I shook my head. "You don't have to do that. If you just tell me where the kitchen is, I can make my own food."

"Absolutely not," she said, crossing her arms over her chest, "if Loretta Ricci finds out that you've refused her food, I'll never hear the end of it. She would take it as a personal insult and never forgive me for allowing you to make your own dinner."

"I don't want to upset anyone," I replied. "Thank you for letting me know."

Bianca winked at me. "Don't you worry, I'll make sure to prepare you for how things work around here. It can be a little overwhelming at first, but you'll get the hang of it."

"Right," I said, "is there anything else I should know? Don't get me wrong, I've got a million questions. I don't even know where to start."

She glanced around quickly, almost as if to make sure no one was watching. "Listen, I shouldn't be telling you this, but I like you, Paige. You're a nice girl." She paused, looking around again. "Just keep your distance from Ingrid."

"Who is Ingrid?" I asked.

"She manages the household affairs," Bianca whispered, "but she fancies herself more Mr. Kingston's wife-to-be than a member of his staff."

"Is there anything going on between them?" I replied.

She shook her head. "No, nothing at all. But trust me, by the way she looks at him, it's just a matter of time until she makes her move. And when that day comes, we'll all be in deep trouble. She wants this place and Mr. Kingston to herself. Just watch out…you never know what might happen."

Bianca began to walk away, but I followed her. "Just one more thing, why was my position open in the first place? Did a vacancy just happen to open up?"

"The last girl, well, she got scared off," Bianca said.

I watched as she disappeared down the hallway

before closing the door to my room and locking myself inside. This place kept getting stranger by the minute. And although I had never been afraid of the dark, I wasn't sure that when night came, I would have the courage to turn the lights out.

Chapter Four

ON THE DOTTED LINE

Brea

As soon as Evan answered his phone, I launched into my speech. "Why didn't you tell me I would have to move into his giant, somewhat-creepy house? And what is up with his obsession with red? This place looks like it belongs to an evil mastermind! How exactly did you fail to inform me of these EXTREMELY important details before sending me on my way to walk into his office and look like a totally unprepared idiot! He probably thinks I'm completely incompetent, and I haven't even decided yet what I think of him."

"Oh," Evan whispered, "I didn't send you that email?"

"What email?!" I replied.

"I thought I sent you a document with all this information. Cain emailed it to me, and I tried to forward it to you," he said.

"Well, you definitely didn't," I grumbled.

"I'm really sorry, Brea," Evan whispered. "I thought you were prepared. He's kind of eccentric, but he's not dangerous or anything."

"Eccentric doesn't even begin to cover what he is," I replied.

"Look, I'm really sorry, Brea. I promise I am, but I've got to go. Okay?" Even said.

My head was pounding with what I assumed was going to be a killer headache. "What could be more important than this situation you and Enzo have gotten me into? This is kind of a big deal."

"Enzo got a date, and he wants my help getting ready," he replied.

"Fine," I groaned, "but if anything else crazy happens, I'm calling you back."

"Good luck, Brea," Evan said, ending the call.

I began rubbing my temples, wondering how I was going to combat this awful headache. Before I could go and search the bathroom cabinets for painkillers, a knock sounded at the door. After everything that had happened in just a few hours, I wouldn't have been surprised if an alien was standing out in the hallway. Nothing was out of the realm of possibility. There was no alien on the other side of the door, though. Instead, Cain stood there towering over me in only a pair of gym shorts.

It was impossible to prevent my eyes from going wide at the sight of his bare chest and heavily muscled abdomen. Cain's hair was a bit disheveled, and there was sweat glistening on his forehead. I couldn't stop my gaze from traveling over his defined biceps and broad shoulders, then all the way down the rest of his body. Cain cleared his throat, and my face immediately turned a bright red.

"I just wanted to see that you got settled in," Cain said.

I nodded quickly. "Yes, my rooms are lovely. Thank you."

"Do you like books?" he asked.

"Oh, yes. There's a nice selection to choose from," I replied.

He wiped the sweat from his brow. "Good. They were all ordered for you, so whichever ones you like, you're free to take when you move out."

My jaw dropped. "All of these books were bought for me?"

The hint of a smile crossed his face. "Where did you think they came from?"

I blushed. "Oh, well, I just assumed they were from some other part of the house."

He shook his head. "No, they're just for you. There is a library downstairs if you want a wider selection."

I tried to hide the excitement in my voice. "You have a library?"

Cain nodded. "Yes, and a gym, pool, and theater."

Of course, he had those things; he was

ridiculously rich. What had I expected from a man with endless funds and no one but himself to spend money on? I was surprised he didn't have a private spa, too. Maybe he did, and I just didn't know about it.

"You're free to use them, of course," Cain said.

"Oh, thank you…I'll think about it," I replied.

"Have you had a chance to sign those papers I gave you?" he asked.

I shook my head. "Not all of them, I only just got here."

Cain raised his eyebrows. "It's almost time for dinner."

My eyes grew wide. "I must have lost track of time. I'll look at them now."

He nodded. "Good, I need them before you go to sleep."

"Um, why?" I asked.

Cain leaned against the doorframe, staring down at me. "Policy, Ms. Paige."

"Right," I whispered, "I'll get on that."

"Thank you," he replied before turning to open the door on the other side of the hall.

"Wait," I said, "why are you going in there?"

He looked at me with amusement in his eyes. "Because it's where I sleep and shower, Brea. Typically, that's where one goes after exercising."

"You mean, your room is across from mine?" I replied.

Cain smirked. "Stating the obvious, are we?"

"Sorry, I'm just...surprised," I answered.

"Well, now you know," Cain said, stepping inside his room.

Without another word, he closed the door behind him. To my surprise, I didn't hear the lock slide into place. *Of course not*, I thought, *it's his house.* Yet all I could think about was how entirely strange it was that he had selected this room for me, and that he was so insistent that I sign the papers as quickly as possible. What was so important about them that he couldn't wait until morning? I had already filled out all the forms, except the NDA. Bianca had interrupted me before I'd had a chance to look at it, and I'd spent the next few hours exploring the rooms without keeping track of time.

I hurried back over to my desk, eager to read this all-important document. The first page looked normal. It explained exactly what a nondisclosure agreement was and the consequences of breaking one. I almost panicked when I saw just how much money Cain could sue me for if I violated it. The second page was a bit more interesting. It detailed all of the things I was required to keep private, including: "Any events or conversations that occur in or around Mr. Kingston's private quarters, or in any other location within the Kingston residence." What exactly did that involve? Was I not allowed to tell my friends what Cain ate for breakfast, or was there something else implied within this vague requirement?

If Evan and Enzo hadn't put much thought into the fact that Cain was going to dictate where I lived and what clothes I wore, I was certain that they hadn't really considered the significance of this NDA, either. Then again, maybe I wasn't supposed to discuss it with them. Would that be a breach of contract? Cain certainly wasn't making things easy for me with all the mystery that seemed to surround him.

Unfortunately, I kept finding myself distracted by just how handsome he looked without a shirt on. I knew it was wrong to think of him that way. After all, he was my boss. But still, after the way he'd leaned against my doorframe, looking down at me with such confidence in his eyes, I couldn't help but think about seeing him like that again. He was the type of man who could have anything he wanted, no questions asked. Maybe he'd workout every day, and I could lurk in the hallway long enough to catch a glimpse without him noticing. *No,* I thought, *that would be wrong, Brea.* I tried to shake the thought from my mind, not wanting anything to mess up this job. I was here for the money and nothing else. Cain was paying me extremely well, which was the only reason I would tolerate these crazy requirements. Nothing else mattered.

Chapter Five

COMFORTABLE

Brea

I decided to shower away my worries before dinner, hoping it would provide me with a clear mind. And due to the luxurious bathroom I had been given, I was not at all disappointed. The water pressure and temperature were absolutely perfect, and the expensive soaps and shampoo I had discovered made my body smell like a rose garden in full bloom. After stepping out of the water, I wrapped a fluffy towel around my body and began to brush out my hair. Since Bianca had said she would deliver dinner to my room, I decided there was no reason to put work clothes back on. Instead, I wandered into the closet and examined the wide variety of pajamas available.

It would have taken far too long for Bianca to have put these clothes in here today, especially since I had arrived before noon. And even if she could have managed it, no stores would have delivered them between the time I left Cain's office and when I arrived here. These clothes, including all the red dresses, had been here for who knows how long. On top of that, how had Cain even known my size, that I liked reading, and that my favorite color was pink? He must have asked Evan and Enzo, and just like everything else, they had apparently forgotten to tell me. Cain had obviously been preparing for my arrival for a while. No matter how hard I tried, I simply couldn't understand why he would invest so much money into a personal assistant, especially one who was only going to work for him for three months. What was the point?

That puzzle was going to take more information than I currently had to solve, so I turned my attention to finding the most comfortable article of clothing I could. My plan was to simply slip out of my room for less than a minute to slide the paperwork under Cain's door, then escape back inside. After throwing on a pair of cotton pajama pants and a loose white t-shirt, I took the manila envelope and stepped into the hallway.

"Well, you're not what I was expecting," a female voice said.

In such a quiet house, her chiding comment seemed to boom. I looked up to find a tall woman with long blond curls, cherry-red lips, and startling green eyes. The navy blue dress she wore displayed her large chest and wide hips. She had a feline smile and a stillness of demeanor that made me shiver.

She tilted her head to the side. "We haven't been introduced. My name is Ingrid Burke. I manage

Mr. Kingston's household affairs. And you are Brea, I presume?"

I nodded, attempting to sound far more confident than I was. "Yes, I'm Brea Paige. If I may ask, what were you expecting?"

Ingrid smirked. "Well, not a little girl wearing pajamas."

My cheeks turned red. "I'm nineteen, and I wasn't expecting to run into anyone."

She looked down to examine her perfectly styled nails. "I'll give you a piece of advice, Brea. Never lower your guard in this house. And always, always, expect the unexpected."

Ingrid turned her back, her curls bouncing as she began walking down the hallway. I sighed, wondering how I had managed to let that introduction go so horribly wrong. Bianca was right, Ingrid certainly wasn't someone I'd want to be spending my spare time with. She was like a sour grape at the bottom of the bag that had turned mushy and rotten, except much prettier.

As I leaned down to slide the envelope under Cain's door, I heard the doorknob turn. I silently vowed never to step foot outside of my bedroom in anything other than business attire again for as long as I lived in this house.

"You are aware that you're allowed to knock, right?" Cain asked.

I stood up, attempting to hide the embarrassment on my face. "I'm sorry, I didn't mean to bother you. I just wanted to return these."

Cain took the envelope from my hands. "Thank you, Brea. I appreciate your timeliness."

"Well, it's the first task you gave me, so I didn't want to make any mistakes," I replied.

The hint of a smile crossed his face. "I overheard your conversation with Ingrid. Don't take offense, she doesn't mean any harm." He glanced down at my pajamas. "You look…comfortable. No one ever does around me, but…I like it. Always being perceived as the big bad wolf gets old."

I bit my lip. "Oh, thank you."

A moment of silence passed. "I'll see you tomorrow, Ms.Paige."

"Right, of course," I replied.

"Goodnight, Brea," Cain whispered, closing his bedroom door behind him.

I hurried back into my room, determined never to let Cain Kingston ever see me so startled again.

Chapter Six
BEAUTIFUL WOMAN

Brea

The next morning, I woke up at six o'clock sharp. By the time Bianca knocked on my door with breakfast, I was already dressed for the day in a red A-line dress with black stockings and sling-back heels. My makeup was done to perfection, and my hair was pulled back nicely in a smooth chignon. This was my first real day working with Cain, and I wouldn't give him or Ingrid the opportunity to criticize my appearance. If he wanted me to wear red every day for some irrational reason, I would, because what he was paying me was worth far more than the lack of variety in my wardrobe.

When I opened my bedroom door and stepped out into the hallway, Cain was leaning against the wall waiting for me. He wore a black dress shirt with a charcoal grey suit and a dark red tie. As he examined my attire, a hint of approval peeked through his stoic persona.

"Are you ready?" he asked.

I nodded. "Absolutely."

I followed Cain down the hallway, having to increase my speed to keep up with his casual stride. He was so much taller than me that it was almost annoying. But despite my fervent protest, the casual confidence he exuded caused a flurry in my abdomen. I silently scolded myself, trying to remember exactly why I was following this absurdly powerful man around like a lost puppy. Despite what my more romantic instincts might have desired, I was absolutely not in this position to fall in love with Cain Kingston.

We walked silently outside and up to the waiting car. To my surprise, Cain stepped aside and allowed Wolf to open the door to the Mercedes. As soon as I had situated myself inside, Cain slid into the seat beside me. For some reason, I hadn't expected to ride to work with him. But when I considered it, it did seem logical. After all, we were going to the same place. Still, he seemed like the type of man who preferred solitude.

"Straight to the office, sir?" Wolf asked.

Cain nodded. "Yes."

I couldn't help but be surprised when a privacy screen slid down from the ceiling, separating the back seat from the front. Being in such a small and confined space with Cain made goosebumps appear on my arms. I looked away in an attempt to avoid any potential eye contact. If I had known the way his presence would impact me, I might never have taken the job. He wasn't just easy on the eyes. Cain was the epitome of all things masculine and intoxicating.

"I have meetings all day," Cain said, his voice calm and collected. "You'll sit behind me during them and listen carefully. If I need anything like coffee or water, you'll be sent to retrieve them. The meetings will likely be extremely boring, but try not to let your mind wander."

"Of course," I replied.

"Do you have any questions?" he asked.

It was hard not to be distracted by his silky smooth voice. Somehow, I was able to maintain a professional tone. And yet, there was a small part of me that seemed to sense that Cain knew exactly what I was thinking. That made the heat in my abdomen so much worse.

I looked directly at him, attempting to portray a blank expression. "Will that be the extent of my responsibilities? Am I just here to get coffee whenever you need a dose of caffeine?"

He almost smiled. "You're here to do whatever I require, Ms. Paige. That is the point of a personal assistant. I have a secretary to answer phone calls and emails–that's not your job."

It made me slightly annoyed that my summer would be spent sitting silently and fetching snacks instead of doing something important. But when I reminded myself that this wasn't some sort of unpaid internship, my irritation faded. If nothing else, I had the opportunity to observe the everyday routine of a powerful businessman. It could be helpful in my future career. Besides, it was good for my resume.

"Is that agreeable with you, Brea?" Cain asked.

I nodded. "Of course, I just want to make sure I'm doing a job worth what you're paying me. I want to be useful."

A look of surprise crossed Cain's face for the briefest of moments. "Don't worry about the money. It's nothing."

My jaw almost dropped. "What you're paying me is likely more than I'll make in a year after graduation. It's certainly not nothing."

Cain leaned back against his seat. "It's an insignificant amount to me, Brea. Enough about the money, I don't want to discuss it further."

It took every bit of willpower I had to close my mouth and keep it shut. I looked down at my manicured nails, trying to avoid focusing on how Cain continued to stare at me, his eyes roaming up and down my body. I was acutely aware of just how close he was, and though my imagination could have been running wild, I got the feeling that he was tempted to lean over and close the gap between us. But that was probably just my hormones talking.

After a tense car ride, we finally arrived at our destination. When Wolf opened the door, Cain motioned for me to exit first. I exited the vehicle as gracefully as possible, which was rather difficult in a tight dress and heels. After Cain stepped out of the car, he headed directly for the front door, clearly intending for me to follow.

When we walked into Kingston Headquarters, there was an immediate shift in the atmosphere. People parted like the Red Sea as Cain walked past them toward the elevators. Everyone stared silently as we passed them, watching as the most powerful man in the building, and maybe the entire city, made his way to what I was starting to believe was more of a throne room than an office. And by the way, all of the women looked at Cain, and it certainly started to feel like he was much more of a dark, mysterious prince than a businessman. Honestly, I couldn't blame them.

When we finally reached Cain's office, I felt like I could breathe again. He seemed entirely unbothered. Did people always act so…terrified around him?

Almost as if he could read my mind, Cain answered. "They're not silent out of fear, Brea. It's about respect. I pay them well and give them fair working conditions. In return, they respect me. It's as simple as that."

"Everyone always seems terrified of you," I replied.

He almost smiled. "I have been told that I can be a bit intimidating."

I rolled my eyes. "The understatement of the

year."

"It's time for the first meeting of the day. Are you ready?" Cain asked.

I nodded. "Yes."

"Good," he replied, before leading me to a large conference room down the hall.

When we entered the room, every seat except one at the long wooden table was occupied. As expected, everyone grew silent as Cain pulled out his chair and sat like a king on his throne. Directly behind him was another chair, which I decided must have been for me. There were no other secretaries or assistants in the room, but given that Cain was the most important person in the whole building, it wasn't exactly shocking that he would have one when no one else did. He was also the youngest person at the table, which didn't surprise me. Cain was exceptionally successful for someone his age.

"Well, let's get started," he said.

The only other female in the room, a woman perhaps in her late sixties, took that as her que. "I have the new designs you requested, sir."

"Wonderful," he replied, "let me see."

The woman slid a large, black velvet box across the table to Cain. As he opened it, I tilted my head to the side to see the contents. Slowly, he pulled out three different necklaces, each of which I imagined was worth more than a small house. They were definitely meant for people in a different tax bracket than me.

"Our team spent weeks perfecting them, sir," she said.

"They are exquisite, Mabel," Cain replied. "I'm particularly fond of this one."

My eyes grew wide as he held up a delicate choker necklace adorned with shimmering blue sapphires and countless round diamonds. It was certainly the most beautiful piece of jewelry I had ever seen. Up until now, I hadn't known that Cain was actually involved in the design aspect of the company. I had assumed he managed the money, business deals, and other things of that nature. But it actually made sense that he took an interest in their products. After all, this was still a family business. His grandfather and uncle were both incredibly talented jewelers who, through hard work and determination, had managed to start a company that made their family extraordinarily wealthy. It would be strange if Cain didn't know at least a little about the art of design, given that it was his family's trade.

"Although I believe it would look even more stunning around the neck of a beautiful woman," Cain remarked.

Mable nodded. "Yes, sir. I can bring in a model if you'd like."

He shook his head. "We already have one. Brea, come here."

My eyes grew wide. "Sir?"

Cain turned to face me. "I want you to try this on."

Everyone was staring at me, and it was hard to keep my voice steady. "Okay."

I walked over to him. Cain stood, once again towering over me. "Turn around."

I tried not to shake as he reached around to fasten the choker around my neck. Never before had I felt so self-conscious. Everyone in the room was focused solely on me. I heard the clasp click shut, and Cain stepped away.

"There," he said, "absolutely gorgeous."

I was fully aware that my cheeks were as red as a cherry tomato. This was the exact opposite of what I had expected this day to be like. The impression I had been given was that I would be practically invisible during these meetings, but that certainly wasn't the case. Not anymore, at least.

"Mabel, I'd like you to make another necklace identical to this one to put out on the floor for display. However, do not sell it. This piece, and the design, now belong to Ms.Paige," Cain ordered.

Mabel's eyes looked like they might pop out of her head. "Sir, I don't understand. The cost in materials for this piece was exponential. I didn't realize it was a personal gift. If you'd like, I could make a less expensive replica…"

"Did I stutter?" Cain interrupted. "You heard your instructions, Mabel. This is not up for discussion. Do exactly as I said, or we are going to have a problem."

Mable nodded. "Of course, sir."

Cain glanced at me. "Brea, you may sit back down."

It took every bit of concentration I had not to protest what Cain had just done, but I wasn't going to argue with my boss in a room full of other people. So like a lamb, I retreated back to my chair and tried to melt into the wall. Given that everyone was still staring at me, it certainly wasn't working.

"Now, let's move on to marketing," Cain said.

The entire room shifted focus back to him, but my mind couldn't seem to process a word of what he was saying. As my heart pounded in my chest, I couldn't help but wonder exactly what I had gotten myself into.

Chapter Seven

TERRIBLY ATTRACTIVE, MYSTERIOUS, AND ALLURING

Brea

Around noon, Cain led me back to his office. He hadn't spoken a word to me since the first meeting of the morning. That was probably a good thing, since I had no idea how I was supposed to respond to what he'd done.

When Cain sat down behind his desk, his eyes met mine. "We have a short break now, Brea. Lunch will be brought up in a few moments. I took the liberty of ordering for you."

I clasped my hands together in an effort to stop them from shaking. "Sir, I truly appreciate everything you've done for me so far, but I simply can't accept this necklace. It's…extravagant…and completely unnecessary."

Cain leaned back, raising his eyebrows. "And why exactly are you so opposed to accepting a gift?"

"I haven't done anything to earn this," I replied.

I decided not to mention the fact that accepting any gift from him, especially a piece of jewelry, felt wrong. It was entirely unprofessional and had to violate all sorts of rules about workplace conduct.

He tilted his head to the side. "You're afraid of what people might say."

I blushed, looking down at the carpet. "Sir, I'm already living in your house. People might get the wrong idea."

Cain's face grew serious. "I don't care what anyone else says about the relationship between you and me, Brea. Gossip is a waste of time. But if someone in this building makes a rude comment or even so much as looks at you unkindly, you will tell me immediately. Is that understood?"

I nodded. "Yes, but…"

Cain frowned. "Discussion over."

I wanted to protest, but some small little voice inside my mind urged me to comply. *He's your boss, Brea,* I thought. I closed my eyes. *Don't fight it, just let him win.* A knock sounded at the door, forcing me out of my contemplation.

Olive stepped inside, a wide smile on her face. "Brea, so nice to see you again!"

I attempted to smile back. "Same here."

She walked over to Cain's desk, placing a large paper bag in front of him. "The delivery guy was actually on time today. Crazy."

Cain gave her a tight smile. "Thank you, Olive. That'll be all."

She gave me a little wave before leaving the room and closing the door behind her. Part of me hated seeing her go. Being alone with Cain made me feel particularly…vulnerable. It seemed safer when someone else was around. When it was just the two of us, the energy seemed to shift. Though he tried to appear unfazed by anything or anyone, I could tell that Cain felt the difference, too. That made it all the more terrifying.

"Come here," he commanded.

I walked over to his desk, glancing down at the contents in the paper bag. "Pizza?"

The hint of a smile threatened to cross his face. "Yes."

"I just…I never imagined you eating fast food," I replied.

He pulled two boxes out of the bag, handing me one. "Well, you don't have to use your imagination now."

I took the box and retreated to the couch across from his desk. "Do we eat here?"

He nodded, taking a bite of pepperoni pizza. "It's likely the only peace and quiet you'll get all day, so I'd recommend you try to enjoy it."

We ate in silence. Cain seemed perfectly content, but I could barely manage to get a single slice down before I finally made myself stop. The pizza was absolutely delicious, but for some reason, the only thing I could think about was him. Every time our eyes met, I felt my heart flutter. *Don't ruin this, Brea. You need a job, not a situationship. He would likely toss you aside the moment he found someone better.* I shook my head, trying to find what little common sense was left somewhere in my brain.

After what felt like forever, Cain finished eating. "Not hungry?"

"Nerves," I replied.

"You have no reason to be anxious, Brea. I'm going to take care of you," he replied.

"Yeah, that's kind of what I'm worried about," I whispered.

He frowned. "Explain."

I bit my lip. "I…I don't know how to react to all of this."

"Then don't," he replied.

"What?" I asked.

"Stop worrying, Brea. As long as you work for me, just follow my instructions, and don't overthink things," he said.

This was not the man Evan and Enzo had described to me. Before starting this job, I had expected to be working for a ruthless, greedy, egotistical businessman with no capacity for generosity or thoughtfulness. Instead, I had been confronted with a terribly attractive, mysterious, and alluring man who made my heart beat so fast I thought it might pound out of my chest. How was I supposed to survive the summer working for him without allowing myself to fall hopelessly in love? The only thing I knew was that this job was a whole lot more than I had bargained for.

Chapter Eight

REGRETS

Brea

"I can not believe Evan and Enzo let you walk into this completely unprepared!" Mila shouted, making me jump.

"Shhhh," I whispered, "his room is right across the hall."

Mila had come over in the early evening to see how my first day working with Cain had gone. Just like me, she was completely shocked, and perhaps horrified, that I had been thrust into this situation with absolutely no warning. Her reaction made me feel a little less crazy.

"You and me both," I grumbled.

Suddenly, a look I knew all too well crossed Mila's face. In less than a second, she went from outraged to scheming. I braced myself for whatever sort of crazy plan she was about to propose. No matter what it was, I knew it would only make my problems worse.

"You said you're attracted to him, right?" she

asked.

Oh no, not this again. The last thing I wanted to think about was how fast Cain made my heart beat, or how badly I had been tempted to lean over and kiss him on the car ride back. I needed to do everything I could to get those thoughts out of my mind.

I nodded. "Yes, and that's a bad thing. He's my boss, Mila."

She rolled her eyes. "I don't think traditional standards of professionalism apply here, Brea. He had you move into his house, is dictating what clothes you wear, and just gifted you a piece of jewelry more expensive than any I own. He's clearly not a stickler for rules."

"That may be so, but I don't need to be involved in a scandal," I replied.

"What would be so bad about it?" she asked. "You're both adults, neither of whom is married or even in a relationship, and there's obviously chemistry between you. I see no scandal here, only a love story."

She was right, sort of. Aside from the power imbalance, there was no real reason a relationship between Cain and me would be wrong. He wasn't tied down to anyone, and neither was I. We were both seemingly on the market. Still, if anything happened between us, people would probably think I had been coerced or manipulated. I didn't want Cain to be vilified in that way, and I didn't want to be perceived as weak.

"Once again, regardless of anything else, he's my boss. I work for him," I replied.

She smirked. "Are you naive enough to think that no one has ever fallen in love with their boss before?"

People started relationships with colleagues all the time, I knew that. But typically, they were in somewhat similar financial positions . Cain could literally buy anything he wanted, and I used coupons at the grocery store. We were not the same.

"Of course not," I replied. "But he and I, we're from different worlds. He's a billionaire, and I'm…,"

"Perfect," Mila interjected. "You're perfect, Brea. How many times do I have to tell you that you're stunning? Any man would be lucky to have you. And aside from your looks, you're also crazy smart. It's no wonder he wants you."

I frowned. "Look, even if all of that were true, we don't know what he wants from me. Besides, don't you think it's a little creepy how he made sure to learn everything about me before we even met?"

She shrugged. "If I were a billionaire, I'd do the same thing. You can't just go around blindly trusting people when you're someone like him. He needed to do his research. And I'm sure he didn't have to try very hard–Evan and Enzo are blabbermouths."

That was true. It would have been stupid for

him to hire me without any background knowledge. It was likely that no one ever set foot in his office without a background check. He worked in the jewelry business, and there was certainly a large possibility of theft, blackmail, or even kidnapping. Although I doubted it would be easy for anyone to abduct him. If the business world failed him, I had no doubt that he could become a professional athlete. His body was… perfection.

I threw myself down into the luxurious bed, staring up at the tall ceiling. "This is just supposed to be a summer job, Mila."

Her face turned serious. "I know that was your plan , but things change. When life gives you something special, like the connection you have with Cain, why throw it away? You've always been one for rules and restrictions, but maybe it's time to finally let yourself live. You don't have to spend your entire life fighting some imaginary battle."

She truly didn't understand. Unlike Mila, I'd had to fight for everything I got in life. I already felt like I didn't deserve this job. If I hadn't been friends with Evan and Enzo, I never would have gotten it. It would take me a while to move past the guilt. I wanted to prove to everyone that I was capable of doing things on my own, and getting handouts certainly wasn't going to make people view me as strong and independent.

I closed my eyes. "Mila, the moment I let myself

fall in love with him, he'll decide I'm nothing more than a desperate girl out for his money. There's no other way it could go."

"That's a possibility," she replied, "but if you don't at least try, you might spend the rest of your life wishing you had."

I sighed, letting her words soak in. There was truth to what she was saying, but it scared me. I couldn't bear the thought of letting myself fall totally in love with him only to face rejection and defeat. For all I knew, Cain treated all of his assistants the same way. It was entirely likely that I was no different from anyone else in his mind, and that any interest he had was temporary and superficial. He might have thought I was pretty, but that wouldn't mean anything the moment a more beautiful girl caught his eye.

"I'll think about it," I replied.

She squeezed my hand. "Good, that's all I'm asking. I just don't want you to have any regrets, Brea."

I smiled. "I know."

She leaned down, giving me a tight hug. "Now, does this place have any kind of room service? I'm starving."

Chapter Nine
FIGHTING CHANCE

Brea

Later that night, several hours after Mila left to go home, I heard a knock at the door. I was a bit worried that it was Cain. The possibility that he might have overheard my conversation with Mila was absolutely terrifying. It was likely he already knew I was attracted to him. Who wouldn't be? But I still didn't want him to know I admitted it.

When I opened the door, my fears were confirmed. Cain was leaning against a wall, a small smirk on his face. I bit my lip as my entire face turned a bright red.

"Good Evening, Brea," he whispered.

It was hard to avoid looking into his perfect eyes. "Hi."

His smirk grew wider as he tilted his head to the side. "Do you have plans for tonight?"

I raised my eyebrows. "Um, no, I don't think so."

He almost laughed. "You don't think so?"

"I mean, I don't have plans," I replied.

Cain nodded. "In that case, how would you feel about joining me for dinner?"

A million thoughts raced through my mind. Was he proposing what I thought he was? Was Cain Kingston, my boss, asking me on a date? There was no way. It was obvious that he had overheard my conversation with Mila, but the best thing for him to do would have been to pretend like it never happened. At least, that's what would have been the most professional. But it was beginning to become abundantly clear that Cain wasn't exactly a stickler for rules, at least not for himself.

"Um, do you think that's a good idea?" I asked.

He leaned back against. "Seems like an excellent idea to me."

"In what context would this dinner be?" I replied.

He shrugged, turning around to open the door to his room. "I don't know, I guess we'll figure it out. Be ready in thirty minutes."

The next thing I knew, Cain closed his bedroom door behind him, and I was left standing in the hallway alone.

I spent the next thirty minutes in an absolute panic. What on earth was I supposed to wear? What were his expectations? This was all Mila's fault, and that was exactly what I was going to tell her the next time we spoke. By the time I finally decided on an outfit, my closet looked like it had been hit by a hurricane. Clothes were strewn all over the floor, and at least a dozen different pairs of shoes were tossed about. In the end, I opted for a floor-length sheath dress with a slit that rose just above my knee. Like most of the other clothes Cain had gifted me, it was a dark red color that paired nicely with the black stilettos I selected. I also wore the outrageously expensive sapphire necklace Cain had demanded I accept earlier in the day, knowing he would likely be disappointed if I didn't. Rather than let my hair remain in the updo I had put it in for work, I decided to let my long locks down in a waterfall of chocolate curls that stood out against my pale skin. I felt silly putting so much thought into exactly what Cain would want me to wear. It had been years since I cared so much about a man's perception of me. Not because I wasn't interested in love, but because they never seemed to want anything more than a fling. That wasn't what I was interested in, which is part of why I was so concerned about falling in love with Cain. There was simply no way he wanted anything serious.

When I glanced down at my phone, I realized I was running late. I rushed to the door and threw it open far less gracefully than intended. Cain continued to stare down at his watch, ignoring my dramatic entrance. I could tell he was acutely aware of my anxiety, though.

"Well, Ms. Paige, you certainly know how to keep a man waiting," he said.

His appearance stunned me speechless. Cain would have looked handsome wearing a burlap sack, but in his midnight-black tailored suit, he was otherworldly. And from the look in his eyes, he knew just how breathtaking his appearance was.

"I…I'm sorry," I replied.

He held out his arm. "Well, come on then, Cinderella. If we wait too long, you might turn into a pumpkin."

My hand was shaking as I gently placed it on his arm. We made our way down to the dining room in silence. Cain appeared completely calm, which made me even more anxious. It made me feel like a silly young girl enamored by her older brother's best friend.

When we reached the dining room, Cain pulled out a chair for me across from his. Two plates of food were waiting and ready. Once I smelled the perfectly cooked steak and roasted vegetables, my mouth immediately began to water. I hadn't realized just how hungry I was until I sat down.

For the first few minutes, we ate in total silence. It seemed like Cain was trying to make me squirm. With each bite I took, I could feel his eyes on me. Even though he didn't say a single word, I felt like I was being interrogated.

"What is this, Cain?" I asked.

His eyes glistened mischievously. "A steak, Brea."

I frowned. "Not the food. This whole... situation."

Cain set his utensils down and stared at me. "What do you want it to be?"

I sighed. "You heard my conversation with Mila."

He nodded. "I did."

"Are you trying to embarrass me?" I asked.

"No, but you do look adorable when your face turns bright red," he replied.

I frowned. "I'm sorry for what I said. I never intended to make things awkward between us. I just want to do my job."

"Don't apologize," he said, "I'm actually quite glad I happened to be walking by at the exact right moment. It makes me feel much less guilty for what I'm about to do."

My eyes grew wide. "What exactly is that?"

He leaned back in his chair. "Ask you to date me."

"What?" I whispered.

He smirked. "I don't like repeating myself, Brea."

My heart began pounding in my chest. "Mr. Kingston, I'm flattered, but you're my boss. It would be completely inappropriate."

"You would say yes if I wasn't your employer?" He asked.

I glance down at the table. "Well, I…"

Cain nodded. "I had a feeling this would be your objection. Thankfully, this problem can be easily solved. As of now, I'm terminating your internship."

My jaw dropped. "No, you can't. Please, sir. I don't have another job."

Cain held up his hand. "Let me finish, Brea." He slid an envelope across the table to me. "Open it."

Not knowing what else to do, I followed his command. When I saw what was inside, my hands began shaking. I could feel Cain's eyes on me, watching my every move.

"In case you're too stunned to read, that is a donation of seventy-five thousand dollars to New Leaf Preschool. That is what you're planning on calling it, right?" he said.

I looked up at him, my eyes beginning to water. "I…I can't take this. I haven't done anything to earn it."

Cain shook his head. "No, but the disadvantaged children you're going to help deserve it. Your dream is an admirable one, Brea. Children, regardless of their background, should be provided with a good education."

"How did you know?" I asked.

"It's the only reason I agreed to hire you, love.

You are an extremely intelligent woman, but you're not actually qualified to work for my company. You have no background in the business world. But once Evan and Enzo told me your plans for the future, I knew I wanted to be part of them. I have wealth, but if I don't use at least a small portion of it to help others in need, then I don't deserve to be where I am," he said.

"Are you trying to buy my affection?" I whispered.

He shook his head. "No. If you decide to never speak to me again, the money is still yours. It's a donation to your future business."

"It's going to be a nonprofit," I responded.

He smiled, and the beauty of it almost made me melt. "I'd expect nothing less."

"Why do you care so much?" I whispered.

Cain frowned. "My cousins never told you?"

I shook my head. "No, they didn't."

He nodded. "I'm adopted, Brea. For the first five years of my life, I lived with my drug-addicted mother and her dealer boyfriend. She never told me who my biological father was. Eventually, the courts terminated her parental rights and put me up for adoption. My true parents, the ones who raised me, adopted me shortly after. Without them, I would have nothing. So when I tell you that I care about disadvantaged children, it's not a lie."

"I had no idea," I replied. "I'm so sorry."

"Don't be," Cain said. "Just accept the money without protest. All I'm trying to do is give those kids a fighting chance."

I smiled. "Okay, I won't refuse the money. Thank you."

"You'll also receive the compensation you were promised for the internship," he said. "Don't argue with me, Brea. It's not up for debate."

I nodded. "We'll just think of it as more money for the preschool."

"If that's what it takes to make you accept it, fine," he grumbled.

A moment of silence passed as I contemplated my options. Cain was not at all the man I had believed him to be. Like so much other critical information, Evan and Enzo had failed to mention Cain's troubled past. I knew so many people who had similar experiences to his, but none of them had been as lucky. Most of the kids I grew up with whose parents struggled with addiction had followed the same path. But from my point of view, it was only because they'd never had anyone to help them. I wanted children from all backgrounds to have a decent chance at life. Even if I was only able to help a few, the work would still be worth it.

Now, not only was I physically attracted to Cain, but also emotionally. Despite how everyone described him as being dark, demanding, and cold, he had a good heart. I couldn't help but suspect that some of Cain's hard exterior was a subconscious attempt to prevent himself from experiencing the type of pain and trauma he had lived through as a child all over again. It was completely understandable. He was a sympathetic man, not a villainous one.

"Okay," I whispered.

Hope filled his eyes. "What?"

My heart began to beat faster. "I'll go out with you."

"Just what I wanted to hear," Cain replied.

Chapter Ten
BROKEN

Brea

At around two in the morning, I woke up to the sound of a terror-filled scream. Before I had a chance to think, I immediately jumped out of bed and pulled a fluffy robe over my thin pajamas. The sound was coming from Cain's room. Without a second thought, I ran out of my room and across the hall. Was he hurt? Had someone broken in to harm him?

When I tugged on the handle, I was surprised to find that the door to his bedroom was unlocked. I dashed inside, almost tripping and falling over my own feet. There wasn't time to be embarrassed, though.

"Mr. Kingston!" I shouted. "Are you alright?"

It was then that I noticed he was still in bed, sweat dripping from his face, and every muscle in his body tense. Cain was…having a nightmare. Against my better judgment, I ran over to the bed and began lightly touching his shoulder. It didn't seem to make a difference. Another blood-curdling scream erupted from his mouth. That was when Wolf burst into the room.

The expression on his face was completely neutral…until he saw me. "Brea, you shouldn't be in here. Go back to your room. Now!"

I shook my head. "I'm not leaving him like this."

For a moment, Wolf looked as if he might pick me up and take me out of the room himself. But for some reason, he changed his mind. I turned my attention back to Cain, who still looked like he was in absolute agony.

"He'll wake up eventually," Wolf whispered. "He always does."

My jaw dropped. "This is…normal?"

Wolf nodded. "I tried to tell him not to put your room right across the hall, but he insisted the nightmares had stopped."

As if on cue, Cain screamed in pain. A tear rolled down my face, and my body began to shake. What could I do? How could I make him feel safe?

"Cain," I whispered, "it's okay. I'm here. Shhhh, it's okay. I promise."

Wolf took a step toward me. "Brea, it's no use. You'll only make yourself more upset."

I stared at him. "I'm not leaving. Unless you plan to drag me out of this room kicking and screaming, I suggest you let me try to help him."

Wolf sighed, but nodded in acquiescence. I cupped Cain's face in my hands, gently whispering words of comfort. At first, I thought my actions weren't making a difference, but then his body began to relax. A moment later, his eyes fluttered open. When he saw me, a look of confusion crossed his face, which quickly turned to fear.

"Brea," he whispered, sitting up to take my hands in his, "what are you doing in here?"

I glanced away. "I–I heard you screaming, and I was afraid you might be hurt. I'm sorry for barging in. I didn't mean to intrude on your privacy."

He shook his head. "No, it's okay. I'm not upset." His attention turned to Wolf. "Thank you, Wolf. You can leave us."

Wolf glanced between Cain and me, clearly confused as to what was going on. Cain must not have told him about our conversation over dinner. Was our relationship supposed to be a secret? I wasn't sure exactly how I felt about that.

When Wolf left the room, Cain looked back at me. "Thank you."

I tried to pull my hands away, but he squeezed them tighter. "You should go back to sleep. It's late."

"No," he whispered, "I couldn't sleep now even if I wanted to."

I debated my question carefully. "What were you dreaming about?"

He glanced down. "My biological mother."

"Oh, I'm so sorry," I whispered.

Cain took a deep breath. "Her boyfriend used to beat her. I don't remember much from those years, but the look on her face when he raised his fists is imprinted on my mind. I'll never forget the fear in her eyes, or how helpless I felt when I stood there and watched."

I reached out to touch his face. "You were a child. Don't blame yourself."

"I could have helped her," he whispered.

I shook my head. "Don't think like that. You weren't even old enough to read, let alone defend your mother from a grown man."

He closed his eyes. "One month after they took me away, he-he killed her."

I froze. "Cain, I'm so sorry. I don't know what to say."

Cain wiped the sweat from his forehead. "I'll never forgive myself."

My heart broke for the man before me. He wasn't at all the person I had previously believed him to be. Did Evan and Enzo truly know their cousin? Had anyone ever seen his soul? This must have been the reason for the NDA. Cain would never want anyone, especially people he did business with, to know about his nightmares. He was the type of man who pretended not to have any vulnerabilities or weaknesses, and he did an extremely convincing job. But after tonight, I would never be able to view him the same way. For the first time, I could see who he truly was. And although

I was willing to bet Cain would disagree, it was a good thing.

Chapter Eleven

COLLECT YOU

Brea

The next morning, the house was eerily quiet. I couldn't remember how or when I'd left Cain's room and returned to mine, but it must have been late. When I finally forced my eyes open, the alarm clock showed that it was 10 o'clock. Panic erupted in my mind as I jumped out of bed. But when I glanced down, I saw a note sitting on my nightstand.

> *Brea,*
>
> *I'm sorry for what you had to witness last night. Although my nightmares used to occur frequently, I hadn't had one for a month or so before you arrived, so I hoped they were gone. That was a foolish thought. As you might have guessed, they are among the many reasons I have not pursued a serious relationship with a woman in years. I hope it didn't scare you off completely.*
>
> *Please sleep as long as you'd like. I*

kept you up far too late last night, and you need rest if you're going to make it through the rest of this summer without running away. Since your internship has been terminated, you no longer need to accompany me to work. However, if you still wish to do so, you're more than welcome.

I'll return later tonight to collect you. We're going to a party. Bianca will bring you a dress to wear. Please be ready by eight, and wear the necklace I gave you.

Again, I apologize for last night.
Cain

I set the note down and took a deep breath. At least I wasn't late for work, but that was only because I no longer had a job. Cain and I hadn't actually discussed if I would continue to live here for the rest of the summer, but I had the feeling he didn't want me to leave. Honestly, I had no clue what I was doing. Gaining an incredibly attractive billionaire boyfriend had not been on my summer to-do list. It wouldn't be hard to fall in love with Cain, but I was worried about him breaking my heart.

I spent the majority of my day wandering around Cain's home. There were a few times I almost worried I might get lost. He had everything a person could wish for: a library, gym, pool, theater, and even a small ballroom. There were over twenty bedrooms and twenty-five bathrooms, as well as two separate kitchens and dining rooms. It seemed strange that one man would need so much space, but perhaps he had family and friends who often spent the night. He didn't exactly seem like a socialite, but businessmen sometimes had to be entertainers even if they were the most introverted people on the planet.

Upon entering the library, I felt like Belle from Beauty and the Beast. It was absolutely stunning. Rows upon rows of floor-to-ceiling bookshelves lined the walls. The floors were made of dark marble, and two huge crystal chandeliers hung from the tall ceiling. They let off a golden glow that made the space feel as if it belonged in a fairytale. In the center of the room sat two velvet Chesterfield sofas facing each other with a small coffee table in between.

It was hard to imagine Cain simply lounging about anywhere, but the thought was appealing. The idea of watching him sit and read seemed fascinating. His expressions were usually so carefully guarded, but perhaps when he was reading a good book, they were able to shine through. I wanted to see him smile with a joy that reached his eyes. Sadly, I suspected that didn't happen very often.

Around six o'clock, I returned to my room. Bianca was standing outside the door waiting.

"There you are," she said, "I was starting to

wonder if you got lost."

I blushed. "No, I was just exploring."

She gave me a knowing look. "I had a feeling you were different. I'll be glad when he moves you in here permanently and gets rid of Ingrid."

My eyes grew wide. "Oh, I don't know about that. This is all so…new."

Bianca smiled. "Trust me, this is already more serious than you know. In all the time I've worked for Mr. Kingston, he's never had a romantic relationship. If he wasn't completely star-struck by you, he never would have said anything. He has plans for you, Brea. Just wait."

I glanced down at the dress bag and black box in her hands. "Is that what he wants me to wear tonight?"

She nodded. "Yes, you'll look beautiful. Don't be afraid."

"I just don't understand," I whispered. "Why me?"

"Because you're different," she replied. "Most of the women interested in him are only out for his money. They see a large bank account, not a man."

"I would never pursue a relationship out of anything other than love," I said. "Money has nothing to do with it."

Bianca smiled. "That's why you're so special. He needs a good, honest girl like you."

She handed me the dress bag and box before

giving me one final smile and walking away. As soon as I closed my bedroom door, I immediately unzipped the bag. Inside was a long, mermaid-style silk dress. The dress was the deepest shade of black I could imagine, almost like a starless night sky. After I finished examining the luxurious fabric, I set it down gently on my bed. Next was the mysterious black box. I slid the lid off, revealing two smaller packages inside. I almost rolled my eyes. Cain certainly enjoyed suspense, even if he wasn't present to experience it. The larger box contained a pair of lace-up heels that looked like they would take forever to put on. But after imagining how nice they would look, I decided the effort was worth it. Finally, I set the shoes aside to open the remaining package. It felt light, almost empty. When I removed the lid, my eyes grew wide. Inside were a set of dangling sapphire earrings that looked far more like they belonged on a princess than me. I was almost afraid to touch them. For half a moment, I thought about refusing the gift. Cain certainly would not have liked that, though. And it was clear that he had selected the earrings to match my necklace.

For some reason that I couldn't quite explain, I wanted to make Cain happy. It was somewhat of a compulsion, but it didn't feel unhealthy. The idea of pleasing him simply made me feel satisfied. I wanted to see him smile again, to see his eyes grow wide and his breath catch when he saw me wearing the dress and jewelry he'd selected. Imagining the scenario not only made me feel beautiful but also powerful. The idea that I could potentially make his stoic persona crack was too tempting to pass up. What would it be like if he really laughed, or if a smile spread all the way from his heart to his eyes? I might have been a bit overconfident, but for some reason, I felt like I might have been the only person with keys to unlock those precious secrets that he shielded so well from everyone else.

Chapter Twelve

MINE

Brea

At exactly eight o'clock, Cain knocked on my door. This time, I had made sure to be ready when he arrived. As soon as I stepped out into the hallway, his eyes became clouded with what I knew was desire. It was clear that he was trying to force his expression to remain neutral, but it wasn't working. Knowing that he wanted me gave me a newfound sense of confidence.

"You're stunning," he whispered.

I blushed. "Thank you. You're very handsome."

It was impossible to look away from his flawless three-piece suit, perfectly groomed hair, and sparkling eyes. It didn't matter what Cain wore. He would always look like a man who stepped right out of a romance novel and into real life. Regardless of what Bianca said about most women being out for Cain's money, it was still hard to believe he was single. Even if I had absolutely no idea who he was and just bumped into him on the side of the road, I would have been star-struck. He was just that handsome. It was shocking that he didn't even model for his own company.

"I look like a beggar compared to you," he replied.

I glanced down at the floor, my face growing even more red. "Thank you for the earrings, and the dress, and the shoes, of course."

He gave me a triumphant smirk. "So, you decided not to fight me about them?"

I rolled my eyes. "Well, you didn't exactly give me any details about this party, so I wasn't sure what else to wear."

He held his arm out, and I placed my hand on his elbow. Anxiety coursed through me. Was I totally out of my league? How was I supposed to behave at this party? Would anyone I knew be there?

"Your heart is racing," Cain said.

"I haven't been to a lot of fancy parties," I replied.

"Don't worry," he said, "just stay with me. I won't leave your side."

"What are you going to tell people?" I asked.

He raised his eyebrows. "If anyone asks, which they won't, I'll tell them the truth. You're my lovely date."

"Why do you say no one will ask?" I replied.

Amusement crossed his face. "When you're as wealthy as I am, people don't typically question who the beautiful woman on your arm is. They'll smile at you and then move on. This is a fundraising event, but most people come for networking and socializing. They'll be polite, don't worry. No one wants to be on my bad side."

"Why's that?" I asked.

Cain chuckled. "Because when you have as much money and power as I do, you can destroy anyone's life effortlessly."

I bit my lip. "And...have you done that before?"

His eyes grew serious. "No, but I never hesitate to do what needs to be done."

A chill ran up my spine, and he seemed to notice.

"I would never do anything to hurt you, Brea. Never. Do you understand that?" he whispered.

I nodded. "Yes."

He smiled softly at me, making my heart melt inside my chest. "Good."

We walked the rest of the way to the car in silence. If someone had told me a week ago that I would be going on a date with Cain Kingston, I would have laughed in their face. It was a preposterous concept. I was no one, absolutely no one. I had no money, no power, and I came from a completely average, boring family. There was nothing that made me exceptional in any way. And yet, he seemed drawn to me. Cain could have had any woman he wanted. I had no doubt that he was capable of attracting a supermodel, a genius, or even a European princess. But instead, at least for a few moments, he wanted me.

As we drove to our destination, Cain laced his fingers through mine. His touch felt like fire on my skin. For some reason, the gesture surprised me. It was more…intimate than I had expected. Cain didn't seem like the romantic type, but he was behaving like a true gentleman. I couldn't have asked for anything more.

When we arrived at the party, I could almost hear my heart pounding in my chest. Cai n exited the car first to open my door and help me out. I held onto him like my life depended on it. The venue looked like a palace. I had never seen such a huge house in person. While Cain's mansion seemed absolutely humongous to me, this place was significantly larger. I felt like a fish out of water. No matter what Cain tried to convince me of, I certainly did not belong at a party like this. These people were American royalty.

"Where are we?" I whispered.

"This is the home of Doctor and Mrs. Chopra. Doctor Chopra is a very skilled orthopedic surgeon, and he also comes from an extremely wealthy family. Mrs. Chopra used to be a model for Chanel and Dior, but now she stays home and raises their six children," Cain replied.

I raised my eyebrows. "Six kids? No wonder they have such a big house."

Cain chuckled. "Yes, they certainly have their hands full. They love children, though. All of the money raised from tonight's event will be used to pay for the medical care of children whose families can't afford it."

"That's...wonderful," I whispered. "How do you know them?"

"Well, Mrs. Chopra enjoys the finer things in life, including jewelry. More than a few times, Dr. Chopra has commissioned specialty pieces for her. He pays well. Over the years, we've developed a friendly rapport," Cain replied.

He led me through a beautiful garden full of colorful, blooming flowers. It smelled heavenly. We walked to the backyard, where a large white tent, tables, and a dance floor had been set up. A trio of violinists stood off to the side playing enchanting music. I had been to a few fancy weddings, but this party upstaged them all. There were endless tables of appetizers and finger foods, a champagne tower, a fully functioning bar, and waiters rushing around taking people's dinner orders. I didn't even want to try to imagine how expensive this whole event must have been to organize and put on.

"Are you doing alright?" Cain asked. "You look a little pale."

I nodded. "I'm fine, just feeling a bit out of place."

Cain wrapped his arm around my waist. "Remember what I told you last night, Brea. After I was adopted, it took me years to adjust to this world. It was unlike anything I had ever imagined. Going from having to worry about where my next meal would come from to parties like this was overwhelming. But in time, you'll come to understand that most of these events are not frivolous displays of wealth. They are designed to raise money and give back to the community. Tonight alone, millions of dollars will be donated to help children who would otherwise suffer or even die. The small talk and socializing are worth it."

"You're absolutely right," I replied. "I just have no idea how to act or what to say."

Cain pulled me closer against him. "Just be yourself, Brea. That's more than enough."

He led me over to an Indian couple whom I presumed to be Doctor and Mrs. Chopra. Like Cain and I, they were dressed immaculately. Doctor Chopra had on a three-piece suit similar to Cain's, while his wife wore a long, flowy dress of emerald-green velvet. She was the picture of elegance. Around her neck was a sweetheart-style diamond necklace that shimmered in the candlelight. I was almost sure it was a signature Kingston piece.

Once again, Cain seemed to read my mind. "My uncle designed that necklace. Doctor Chopra purchased it for her as a wedding present ten years ago. "She's worn it to several red carpet events, which has been wonderful free marketing. I believe it's one of her favorite pieces."

As we approached the couple, Mrs. Chopra's gaze shifted to me. "Oh! You must be Brea. How lovely to meet you. I was thrilled when Cain told me he was bringing a date."

I smiled back. "Thank you so much for having me, Mrs. Chopra."

She reached out to take my hands. "Please, call me Isha. No need to be so formal." She motioned to the man beside her. "This is my husband, Anat."

Anat reached out to shake my hand. "So nice to meet you, Brea. And Cain, it's good to see you. I hope the two of you have a wonderful night."

"Thank you, Anat," Cain said before leading me away.

We walked over to an empty table, and Cain pulled out a chair for me to sit in. "See, not so hard. Are you feeling better?"

I smiled. "Yes, very much. I'm surprised at how welcoming they were."

"Not everyone with money is elitist, I promise," he replied. "Now, would you like me to get you a drink?"

"Um, maybe just some sparkling water?" I asked.

He nodded. "Of course. I'll be right back. Don't move."

As soon as Cain left, a waiter walked over and placed two menus on the table. "Good evening, Miss. I'll be back shortly to collect your order."

I smiled at him. "Thank you."

So far, I was certainly the youngest person in attendance. I got that feeling that most of the guests at these parties weren't college students, especially not those from normal, middle-class families. If I weren't certain that Cain would look out for me, I would have been absolutely terrified. Confirming my suspicions, two men, who looked like father and son, sat down at the table across from me. The older man was likely somewhere in his mid-sixties, while his son looked to be around thirty-five.

"Well, hello there!" the older man said.

"Hello," I replied.

"I'm Charles Kline, and this is my son, Ewan. I don't believe I've seen you before. What's your name?" he asked.

"It's nice to meet you, Mr. Kline. My name is Brea. I'm here with Cain Kingston," I replied.

Charles nodded. "Ahh, Kingston. I'm familiar with him. I used to play golf with his grandfather before I had my knee surgery. Good family."

Before I had to worry about what to say next, Cain returned. He handed me my sparkling water and looked over at the men across the table. Cain's eyes immediately grew dark, startling me.

"Charles, I wasn't expecting to see you here," he said.

Charles waved his hand. "Oh, you know I never miss a good fundraiser, Cain. We all have to do our part."

Cain sat down beside me, resting his arm on the back of my chair. His hand reached up, gently twirling my hair between his fingers. Charles frowned.

"So, where'd you find her? She sure is a beauty. You're not willing to share, are you?" Charles asked.

Immediately, I felt like a prize pig being evaluated for auction. Cain immediately sensed the shift in my behavior and lightly ran his fingers along my back. I leaned back into his touch, relaxing a bit. It was remarkable what he could do to me.

"Where is your wife, Charles? Is she talking to you again after your indiscretions?" Cain asked, a hint of violence in his tone.

Ewan's face immediately grew red, and his father's eyes grew red with anger. "That girl was nothing more than a lying gold digger. My wife knows the truth, and so should you. I don't appreciate you bringing it up."

"I wasn't going to," Cain replied, "until you spoke about my girlfriend like she's an object to be lent out and borrowed."

My eyes grew wide. Had he really just referred to me as his girlfriend? And more importantly, why did he look like he was about to stand up and punch Charles? The two men continued to stare at each other in silence, a storm clearly brewing. Even though we were outside, I needed to get some air.

"Excuse me, I'm going to go to the ladies' room," I whispered.

Cain nodded. "Can you find it on your own?"

I smiled at him. "Of course, I'll be right back."

"Okay, take your time," Cain replied, his eyes never leaving Charles.

I stood from my chair and quickly hurried away. Whatever was going on between the two men, I certainly didn't want to get caught up in it. Being involved in drama was something I actively avoided, and this was no exception. If Cain and Charles wanted to have a staring contest, I wasn't going to be part of it. And from the very little information I had just learned, I had a feeling that Charles wasn't the type of man I wanted to be friends with anyway.

After locating one of many doors to the inside of the Chopra home, I quickly found a restroom. Just like the exterior, the interior of the palatial house was stunning. The floors were some sort of exotic hardwood I had never seen before, and the walls were decorated with what appeared to be priceless artwork inspired by classical romanticism. Hanging from the ceiling were dazzling, golden candle-style chandeliers that made the space feel cozy and warm, even though it was by far the biggest house I'd ever been inside.

After closing the bathroom door behind me, I took a long, deep breath. Everything was happening so fast. As creeped out as I was by Charles, the only thing I could think about was that Cain had referred to me as his girlfriend. Was that just to scare Charles off, or had he said it intentionally? I didn't want him to toss around the term without meaning behind it. I was always extremely careful to make sure I thought about relationships before putting a label on them. Cain and I hadn't discussed official titles or what they meant. I knew he wasn't dating anyone else, but that didn't automatically mean I was his girlfriend. After all, we barely knew each other.

Putting those thoughts in the back of my mind, I quickly touched up my hair and applied a new layer of lip gloss. I hadn't put on too much makeup, but I'd done a simple smoky eye to give myself a bit more flair than usual. After making a few more adjustments, I opened the bathroom door.

"Hello, Brea, I thought I might find you here," Charles said.

I was so startled, I almost jumped backwards. "Oh, I'm–I'm sorry if I kept you waiting for the restroom. I tried not to take too long."

He shook his head. "Not at all, I was waiting for you."

"Um, excuse me?" I replied.

He gave me a sickening grin. "You're not really Kingston's girlfriend, are you? In all the time I've known him, he's never had one. No, you're just some piece of arm candy he picked up and decided to parade around."

I frowned. "I don't know exactly what you're trying to imply, but whatever it is is extremely insulting. Now, I'd appreciate it if you'd move so I can go back outside."

"How much is he paying you for the night?" he asked. "I could double it just to see the look on his face."

My jaw dropped. There was no way to turn this conversation around. Every nerve in my body was on high alert. I attempted to move to the right to escape, but Charles grabbed my arm.

My voice began to shake. "Let go of me!"

"Not a chance," he replied.

The next thing I knew, Cain was there ripping me away. Before I had a chance to react, he threw a punch at the older man's face, easily breaking his nose. I flinched as blood splattered all over my dress. Cain wasn't stopping, though. As Charles began to back away, Cain followed him. There was something sinister in his eyes; it almost scared me.

"Don't you ever touch her again," Cain growled. "She is mine! "

For a moment, Charles looked as if he might

retaliate. But with a much younger and stronger man towering over him, he clearly thought better of it. Charles gave a brief nod before beginning to attempt to wipe the blood off his face.

Not knowing what to do, I remained frozen in place. Cain took my hand in his and began quickly leading me down a different hallway to what seemed to be the front door of the house. I almost had to run in my heels to keep up with his hurried pace. As soon as we stepped outside, Wolf appeared.

"Leaving, sir?" Wolf asked.

"Yes, right now," Cain replied.

Wolf nodded. "I can go get the car..."

"No," Cain said, "we'll walk."

As if on cue, I tripped over my dress and stumbled forward, losing one of my shoes in the process. Without hesitation, Cain swept me up in his arms and continued walking. He didn't miss a beat or slow down at all, just squeezed me tight against his chest while following Wolf to the car. I was starting to feel a bit dizzy, probably because I had forgotten to eat anything since breakfast, so I was actually glad he was carrying me. Finally, we made it to the car, and Cain gently set me inside.

As soon as the doors were shut and we were on our way, Cain turned all of his focus on me. "Brea, are you alright? Did he hurt you?"

I shook my head. "No, he-he just grabbed my

arm."

It seemed as if a thunderstorm was brewing in his eyes. "I'll kill him."

I grabbed his hand. "No, Cain, don't say that. Please, it's not a big deal."

"It is a big deal, Brea," he replied. "I should have protected you. I'm so sorry."

I reached up to stroke his face. "Hey, you did protect me. Don't blame yourself."

Cain reached out and pulled me to him. My face was pressed to his chest, and I could feel his heart beating a million miles an hour. As much as the entire incident had shaken me up, it was clear that it had impacted Cain more.

"I will never, ever, let that happen again, Brea. Trust me," he whispered.

I closed my eyes, inhaling the warm aromas of cinnamon and clove. "I do trust you, Cain. Everything is okay."

His hands softly stroked my hair. Cain's touch was gentle, but his expression looked the complete opposite. If he hadn't been cradling me against him, I might have been afraid. But for some reason, I knew that he would never hurt me. Seeing him hit Charles had certainly startled me, but I had been more afraid for the old man than myself. Cain's expression had been absolutely murderous. But thankfully, after Charles had accepted defeat, Cain had backed away.

Maybe this was why I had been warned not to make him angry. Then again, I truly believed that even if I burned his mansion to the ground, Cain would never look at me with that villainous expression.

"Are you sure you're alright?" he whispered.

I nodded. "Yes, are you?"

"I'll be fine," he replied, looking down to examine the blood on my dress.

I bit my lip. "Sorry about that. I'm sure the dress was expensive."

Cain raised his eyebrows. "Why are you sorry? I'm the one who punched him."

I had to stop myself from laughing. "True."

He leaned over to place a soft kiss on my forehead. "I'll make it up to you, Brea. We'll do something together, just the two of us."

I nodded. "Cain, you said something back there."

"I said a lot," he replied, "which part are you referring to?"

I glanced down. "You told Charles I was your… girlfriend."

"I'm sorry," Cain said. "It just slipped out. Did it offend you?"

I shook my head. "No, I don't think so."

Cain's face grew serious. "Listen very carefully to me, Brea. This is your chance to walk away. If you do, I'll hold nothing against you. After tonight's events, I would certainly understand if you wanted nothing to do with my world. But if you decide to stay, if you decide that I'm what you want, there's no turning back. I take extremely good care of what is mine, Brea. But you should know, I am a jealous man, and that will never change. If you decide to pursue this relationship, you will be mine, and I will protect you with everything I have."

There were two little voices in my mind. The first told me to jump out of the car and run far, far away from this man. He had problems, ones that I would likely never be able to fully understand. It was dangerous to become involved with someone who wasn't entirely emotionally stable. But the second voice said that none of those things mattered. I had more chemistry with Cain than with any other man I'd ever met. I was drawn to him like a moth to a flame. Even if he burned me, I couldn't walk away. And he was also kind, at least to me. If I rejected him, I knew that today, tomorrow, or sometime in the future I would look back and regret it. I didn't want to have to wonder what would have happened if I just said yes.

I looked into his eyes, which were once again beginning to look normal. "I want this, Cain. I do. There is every chance that you could break my heart, but I'm going to do it anyway."

"Oh, Brea," he whispered, "it is far more likely that you will break mine."

Cain leaned over, placing his lips against mine. As my eyes fluttered closed, I imagined what it would be like to kiss him every day for the rest of my life. He was not the type of man I had envisioned myself being with, but perhaps he was the man I needed. Cain reached down, wrapping his fingers in my hair and pulling me closer. I didn't protest at all, but instead simply enjoyed the feel of his fiery touch. This was an incredibly dangerous game to play, but I was certainly a ready and willing participant. He was a tsunami I couldn't escape, so rather than try to fight it, I would let myself be taken by the waves.

Chapter Thirteen

CRAZY, COMPLETELY CRAZY

Brea

The next morning, I woke up with a newspaper on my nightstand. The title read: **Charles Kline Money Laundering Exposed**. My jaw dropped. There was absolutely no doubt in my mind that Cain was behind the article. How he had gotten it published so fast, or found out about the money laundering, I had no idea. But it seemed to me that if Cain Kingston wanted to find dirt on someone, he'd certainly be able to.

I had a terrible headache, likely from the chaos and stress of the previous night. I walked to the bathroom, splashed some water on my face, and opened the cabinet in search of Advil. I was an absolute mess. My hair was tied up in a bun on the top of my head, and there were dark circles under my eyes. Hoping they would work some kind of miracle, I took the pills before wandering back into my bedroom to check the time. I could barely keep my eyes open. It was nine o'clock, not as late as I had feared.

Suddenly, the silence was interrupted by

someone pounding on my door. I instantly knew it wasn't Cain; he never knocked like that. Wondering who it could be, I made my way over and slowly opened the door. To my surprise, Ingrid was standing there with a look of pure fury painted all over her face. Although she was an undeniably beautiful woman with her blond curls, cherry lips, and emerald eyes, the snarl she gave me made her look more like a wild animal.

"Move," she demanded before shoving her way inside my room and slamming the door behind her.

"Um, excuse me?" I asked. "What are you doing?"

"I should be asking you that question," she retorted.

I crossed my arms over my chest. "Look, Ingrid, I don't know what I've done to make you dislike me, but this is ridiculous."

"You can drop the innocent little girl act with me," she hissed. "I know exactly what you're doing, and even though Cain might be falling for it, I'm not."

"What on earth are you talking about?" I replied.

She rolled her eyes. "Oh, come on. It was obvious from the beginning. You came here intending to trap him like a fly in a spider's web. I'm not going to let you steal him from me, though. You might have everyone else in this house fooled, but not me."

I shook my head. "You're crazy, completely

crazy."

She took a step forward. "Before you arrived, he was so close to falling for me. I'm not going to let you mess that up!"

"Look, I don't know what was going on between you and Cain before I got here, but it's not really any of my concern. He's clearly interested in me, not you. None of this was my idea, and I didn't intend to step on your toes. But the fact of the matter is, I'm not going to turn down a man I'm interested in just because you're obsessed with him," I replied.

In that moment, she looked like she wanted to kill me. "You're not going to win, do you understand that? He's fascinated with you for now, but he'll move on. Eventually, he'll get tired of how weak and helpless you are."

"Get out of my room," I whispered.

"It won't be yours for much longer," she hissed, storming out into the hallway and slamming my bedroom door behind her.

What had just happened? Ingrid was clearly delusional, and there was no point trying to reason with a crazy person. Bianca was right, I did need to stay far, far away from the blond-haired maniac. She didn't seem to have an ounce of common sense or restraint in her perfectly proportioned body. I couldn't begin to understand why Cain would keep her around, other than that she must have been good at her job and acted totally different around him. Bianca knew the truth, though, so I clearly wasn't the only one to whom Ingrid displayed her true personality to. How she could keep it wrapped up and hidden around Cain was beyond me.

I couldn't even imagine him being with someone like her. Despite his hard exterior, he was a good man. He had passionately defended me last night and had barely been able to restrain himself from knocking Charles completely unconscious. I had a feeling that if the older man had put up a fight, the whole disaster would have been much, much worse. But Cain could be gentle, too. He had held me so tightly on the way home, stroking my hair so softly I almost fell asleep in his arms. And the kiss we'd shared…it had been perfect. His lips were so soft that it had been hard to believe I was kissing the same man who had just broken someone's nose because he had touched me against my will.

I doubted Ingrid really knew who Cain was on the inside. She likely observed the persona he portrayed to the rest of the world and thought he was just as bitter and rotten as she was. I tried not to be too judgmental or critical of other women, because sometimes it really did feel like the whole world was out to get us, but on occasion, a girl came along who was just so nasty I couldn't defend her. Ingrid did not deserve Cain in any way, and I didn't believe he wanted her either. It seemed obvious to me that if he had wanted to date Ingrid, he simply would have told her so. After all, he hadn't hesitated in asking me out.

But still, she made me nervous. Ingrid was clearly determined to get rid of me as quickly as possible. What was she willing to do? The question made me shiver. I didn't like conflict or drama, especially about romantic partners. The best option was simply to let Cain decide what he wanted, and if that was me, then Ingrid would have to accept it.

Chapter Fourteen

MARKED

Brea

"That is wild," Evan said, taking a sip of his latte.

"You're telling me," I grumbled.

Evan, Enzo, Mila, and I had decided to have brunch together and discuss the events of the past few days. For the most part, they had all been stunned speechless. All three of them were looking at me like I was an alien from outer space.

"So what you're saying is that our grumpy, stoic, and potentially machiavellian cousin has basically professed his love to you and defended your honor?" Enzo asked.

I rolled my eyes. "That is not what I said. He and I are just getting to know each other. But, yes, he does seem to be fairly infatuated."

Mila squealed. "This is wonderful, Brea! When you and Cain get married, you'll be related to Evan and Enzo, how perfect."

"Whoa, slow down," I replied. "Cain and I are nowhere close to marriage or anything like that. I don't even know if he wants a family or children, and you know how important that is to me. If he doesn't want kids, it's a dealbreaker."

Mila looked between Evan and Enzo. "Well, give our girl her answers so we can start planning the wedding.

Evan shrugged. "I have no idea if he wants kids. We're not exactly best buddies."

Enzo shook his head. "Same."

Mila frowned. "You know, considering that you're his cousins, I would have expected you to know more. We need background information!"

"It's okay, Mila," I said. "It'll probably come up in conversation at some point. I'm supposed to go out to dinner with him tonight. We'll have plenty of time to talk."

"Is he really being nice to you?" Evan asked, skeptical.

I nodded. "Yes, he is. He's really a lot different than how you described him. After you peel away his outer shell, Cain is hardly a villain. He's vulnerable and…kind. I know most people don't see him that way, but the truth is that he's a good man who just doesn't want others to see his weaknesses. And honestly, that's not the worst flaw to have. He makes me feel beautiful, more so than anyone else ever has before."

"Aww," Mila replied, "you guys are perfect for each other. It's all working out. I knew you were destined to have a fairytale love story. How could someone as sweet and gorgeous as you not find her very own prince charming?"

I rolled my eyes. "Don't get ahead of yourself. This might just be a passing fling. I don't want to get my hopes up and be sorely disappointed."

Evan exchanged a knowing look with Enzo before he spoke. "Mila, Cain doesn't do flings. When he pursues something, he does it wholeheartedly. If he's already calling you his girlfriend, he has no intentions of backing out. And he's not a particularly patient man, either. He won't just wait around indefinitely and leave you wondering about his intentions. I may not know much about my cousin, but I do know that."

"See!" Mila replied. "We finally have some answers. By the way, Brea, I'm glad you're wearing your necklace. It's stunning on you. "

I blushed. "It's still hard to believe Cain actually gave it to me. "

Enzo's jaw dropped. "Oh, Brea. He's marked you."

"What?" I replied, more than a little confused.

Evan nodded. "Cain doesn't just go around throwing jewelry at women he finds pretty. He's not frivolous like that."

"Okay, this is starting to sound creepy," Mila said.

Enzo looked into my eyes with a serious

expression on his face. "Cain intends for you to be his wife, Brea. Years ago, I overheard a conversation he had with our grandfather. Cain said that when he found the woman he wanted to marry, he would give her a sapphire necklace. He chose that stone because when our uncle proposed to our aunt, he gave her a sapphire engagement ring."

Although a million thoughts were running through my mind, I had no idea how to respond. Cain hardly knew me. How would he have made such an important decision so quickly? If he had told his grandfather the significance of the necklace, there was no way he would have decided to give it to me on a whim. Cain knew exactly what he was doing. Perhaps that was why he had been so angry when Charles had grabbed me last night. I reached up to touch the necklace, gently running my fingers across the stones.

"Well, now we certainly have our answers," Mila whispered. "You're going to be Mrs. Cain Kingston, Brea."

"She could say no," Enzo interjected.

Evan reached across the table to take my hand. "I'm sure this is very overwhelming, Brea. Please, don't feel pressured to be with him simply because he's placed a claim on you. You have free will, and if you want to walk away from this, you can. We'll all support you."

"Last night he-he asked me if I was sure. He

asked me if I wanted to be his," I whispered.

"And what did you say?" Mila asked, raising her eyebrows.

I bit my lip. "I…said I did."

Mila smiled brightly, but the boys didn't seem to share her excitement. Instead, they looked like they'd just seen a ghost. Perhaps they were just surprised. Or maybe, despite what I told them, they still didn't believe Cain could treat me in the way I deserved. Were they really so worried that they couldn't even pretend to be happy?

Evan seemed to notice my concern and gave me a soft smile. "We're very happy for you, Brea. Right, Enzo?"

Enzo nodded. "Of course. Whatever makes you happy."

Mila frowned at them. "Oh, come on. Cheer up. Trust her when she says that this is what she wants. For goodness sake, he's your own cousin."

"Let's talk about something else," Evan said. "Enzo, how was your date?"

"Oooo, yes, tell us," Mila added.

As they began discussing Enzo's latest romantic prospects, my mind began to wander. Did I want to be Cain's wife? What would he expect of me if I agreed to marry him? What would everyone think? I knew that my friends would believe I had the best intentions, but would the public think I was only marrying Cain for his money? I didn't want to be seen as a gold digger or a trophy wife. Although I certainly wanted a husband and children, I had just finished my first year of college. I had so much more to accomplish before I was ready to stay home and raise babies. Would Cain accept that? Was it even something he wanted? I had lots of questions, and very few answers. There was only one man I could find out the truth from. Thankfully, I had a dinner date with him later that night.

Chapter Fifteen
WIFE

Brea

My hands were shaking as I zipped up my bright red off-the-shoulder dress. I knew I wouldn't be able to make it through dinner without attempting to make Cain confess to what Evan and Enzo had told me at brunch. In truth, I hadn't been able to think of anything else all day. Unless they were mistaken, Cain wanted me as his wife. While my brain kept telling me to slow down and react rationally, my heart couldn't help but flutter at the idea. It was a lot to process in such a short period of time. I had always wanted to be a wife and mother. Apart from my dream of opening a preschool, having a happy family was my biggest goal. Maybe he had the same desire. And yet, the most pressing question on my mind was why Cain had chosen me. He was constantly surrounded by pretty women, but only one day after meeting me, a completely average girl, he had apparently decided to mark me as his future wife. It wasn't just a rash decision, but also somewhat crazy. Of course, he hadn't told me the specifics of his intentions yet. I assumed he was probably trying not to scare me off. Tonight, he would have to open up and tell me everything.

I took a deep breath, staring at my reflection in the mirror. It seemed impossible to focus on anything except the sapphires hanging from my neck. The gift held so much more significance than I ever would have imagined. But if Enzo had never overheard that conversation years ago, I would have continued believing the necklace was nothing other than a piece of jewelry. There were very few people who actually knew what it meant, but now I was one of them. And as much as I might have wanted to, I couldn't ignore the significance. Unless, of course, he had made it up as some kind of joke to freak me out, but that didn't seem to be the case.

For our date, I had decided to wear a simple pair of ballet flats. As romantic as it had been having Cain carry me to the car, I didn't want to make him do so two days in a row. This evening would be complicated enough without any wardrobe calamities.

"You look beautiful," Cain whispered from behind me.

I almost screamed. "How did you get in my room ?"

He smirked. "The door was unlocked, so I took it as an invitation."

I rolled my eyes. "Well, you just about scared

me to death."

"My apologies, love," he replied.

He looked so handsome in his red dress shirt, black pants, and matching belt. The top button of his shirt was undone, giving him a more relaxed appearance. I couldn't help but let my eyes roam over him, taking in the sight of the man who apparently intended to be my husband. His eyes held a hunger that made me blush, and I instantly redirected my gaze to the floor.

"Are you ready?" he asked. "Wolf is waiting with the car."

I nodded. "Yes."

Cain reached out and took my hand in his. The moment our skin touched, I felt a spark. He was absolutely intoxicating. Whenever I was near him, my senses felt heightened. It was like he made me come alive in a way I'd never experienced before. I wondered if perhaps I had the same effect on him and if that was why he was so infatuated with me.

As we walked to the car, Cain gave me a curious look. "You seem a little stressed. Is everything alright?"

I decided to distract him. "Did you put that newspaper on my nightstand?"

His eyes sparkled. "Yes."

"Are you making a habit of watching me sleep?" I asked.

He almost laughed. "No, although you do look

rather breathtaking wrapped up in all those blankets. It's endearing."

"I'm assuming that article was your doing?" I replied.

Cain squeezed my hand. "I told you he would pay for what he did, and I meant it. I don't make idle threats, Brea. It's not my style. If I say I'm going to do something, I do it. And last night, I promised to protect you. That vow will not be broken, not until the day I die."

I looked up at him. "Mhm, about that..."

Cain leaned down to place a soft kiss on the top of my head. "We'll talk about it at the restaurant. For now, just relax. I want you to have a good night."

The drive to the restaurant was silent, but not uncomfortable. Cain placed his hand on my thigh, gently rubbing the fabric of my dress between his fingers. If there hadn't been about a million questions ready to burst from my mouth, the caring caress might have made me fall asleep. When we finally arrived and were seated at a table, my whole body was buzzing.

Cain had selected a very romantic restaurant. It was authentically Italian with low lighting and delicious aromas floating through the air. It didn't surprise me one bit when Cain took the liberty of ordering for both of us. Actually, I would have been shocked if he didn't. Cain clearly enjoyed making decisions, and he certainly wasn't hesitant about doing so.

When the waiter finally left, Cain leaned back in his chair. "So, I heard you had brunch with my cousins today."

I frowned. "Who told you that?"

He smirked. "I have my sources ."

Of course he did. Cain was a billionaire. It was no surprise that he was spying on me.

"Well, yes," I replied. "It was a very…interesting meal."

He nodded. "I assumed as much."

I looked directly into his eyes, my heart beginning to beat faster. "Anything you'd like to tell me, Cain?"

He chuckled. "Oh, Brea, you certainly get right to the point. I admire that. It's charming."

"Don't beat around the bush," I replied.

"How did Enzo know? I couldn't figure that part out," he said.

I tapped my fingernails on the table. "He overheard your conversation with your grandfather."

"Ah," Cain replied. "So now that you know, how do you feel?"

I took a deep breath. "I don't know, Cain. I never would have imagined that you were eyeing me to be your wife. It's shocking, to say the least."

He frowned. "I'm not eyeing you, Brea. I've decided."

I crossed my arms over my chest. "You can't

make that decision on your own."

He shook his head. "I'm not, last night you agreed to be mine."

"Cain, I agreed to be your girlfriend. I didn't realize marriage was on the table," I replied.

"I assumed you did. I'm not the type of man to date a woman indefinitely and not put some sort of permanent claim on her," he replied.

"You don't even know my middle name," I retorted.

Cain rolled his eyes. "Yes, I do. It's Isabelle."

I frowned. "Well, I don't know yours."

"My full name is Cain Ares Kingston," he replied. "There, now we're even."

"Your middle name is Ares?" I asked, raising my eyebrows.

"I didn't pick it, Brea," he answered.

"There are other important things," I said. "For example, do you want children? And if so, how many would you like? That's very important to me."

I took a sip of water, waiting for his reply.

Cain shrugged. "As many as you'll give me."

I coughed, choking on my drink.

"Are you alright?" he asked, slightly irritated.

I nodded. "Fine."

He frowned. "I plan to keep you as safe as possible, Brea, but that's going to be rather difficult if you insist on threatening your own life every time you consume a liquid."

"You surprised me," I whispered.

"How could that answer possibly be surprising?" he asked.

"I just…didn't expect it," I replied.

He leaned forward. "What exactly would make you think that I didn't want you to carry my children?"

"I–I don't know," I stuttered.

Cain tilted his head to the side. "Now you know the answer."

The waiter returned, placing salad and breadsticks in front of us. He checked with Cain to see if we needed anything else, but Cain quickly shooed him away. When the waiter left, I continued my interrogation.

I looked back at Cain. "What about college? I need to finish school."

He nodded. "I'd expect nothing less. You can commute from home. I'll hire someone to drive and watch over you."

I ignored the part that he had just implied I needed someone to supervise me, like I was a child. We could come back to that later.

"What about the preschool?" I asked. "I won't give up my dream."

"I wouldn't ask you to, Brea. You seem to be under the impression that I want to lock you in your room and never let you leave. That's not at all my intention," he replied.

I frowned. "Then, what do you expect from me? There has to be a catch."

He shook his head. "All I ask is for your undying love and devotion, and for you to take my name. I'm willing to compromise on almost everything else."

I looked down at my nails, desperately trying to remember the other questions I wanted to ask him. He was being so honest with me, I was caught off guard. I hadn't expected him to open up so easily, but it didn't even seem to make him uncomfortable. Even when I thought I was starting to figure him out, Cain continued to puzzle me.

"You look unhappy. Is my age bothering you?" he asked.

"No, Cain, you're thirty, that's not exactly ancient. What I'm wondering is…why do you want me as your wife?" I whispered.

He looked genuinely puzzled. "You are kind, beautiful, empathetic, and intelligent. There is something so innocent and sweet about you that pulls me in. I can't entirely explain it, but what I do know is that you are the only woman who has ever stirred emotions in me like this. I decided the moment I saw you that I was going to pursue you, and I did. Now I've chosen to have you as my wife, and unless you deny your own feelings by standing up and walking out of this restaurant right now, that's the way it's going to be. I won't literally drag you to the altar, Brea. But what I will do is make sure that you decide by your own free will to meet me there."

"How are you so sure I feel the same way about you?" I asked.

He smirked. "You're so easy to read, Brea. It's truly adorable how clueless you are. For example, you blush whenever you see me, you always angle your body toward mine, your heart rate picks up the moment I touch you, and your pupils dilate after looking at me, meaning that your body is releasing dopamine and oxytocin. All of that, darling, means that you are falling in love with me."

Part of me wanted to be irritated that he had just analyzed my behavior like I was some sort of animal in a zoo, but he wasn't wrong. It was hard to argue with the truth. I was fully aware that I was falling in love with him. The problem was that I didn't know exactly what to do about it.

"I don't know what to say," I whispered.

He reached out to run his fingers along my knuckles, causing me to shiver. "You don't have to, love. Your body has already done all the talking. The only thing you have to do is listen to it. You'll find that once you learn to heed your instincts, everything will make so much more sense."

My whole body was tingling, urging me to lean forward and fall into his arms. I pushed my brain aside, focusing solely on my heart. Yes, yes, yes, it urged. I bit my lip, watching as his own pupils began to dilate. Everything he was telling me was true. He was just as enamored with me as I was with him.

"Tomorrow night, you will come with me to meet my parents," he said. "I will introduce you to them as my future wife. Is that alright with you, Brea?"

His words sounded more like a command than a question, but it didn't bother me. In fact, his tone made me feel a little more relaxed. It was as if on some deep level, I knew that things would be alright because he was handling them.

I was barely able to speak. "Yes," I whispered.

He nodded. "Good."

Moments later, our food arrived. We spent the rest of the evening in comfortable silence.

Chapter Sixteen

FATHER AND SON

Brea

The next day, I accompanied Cain to work. The atmosphere was entirely different than when I was there just a few days before. Cain must have sent out a memo, because everyone was calling me 'ma'am' instead of my name. It was a bit odd. Walking through the office, it was almost as if people were afraid of me. But I was following Cain around, so it was probably more likely that they were just nervous around him, and I was an afterthought.

After we had arrived home the previous night, Cain had presented me with a breathtaking cushion-cut diamond ring. The stone was so big, it almost felt heavy on my finger. The weight would certainly take some getting used to. But Cain had been absolutely insistent that I wear it, and I hadn't wanted to refuse him.

Throughout the morning and afternoon, I walked around in a bit of a daze. So much had happened in such a short period of time, but I wasn't upset about it.

For some reason, everything felt right. Was it rational? Absolutely not. Would everyone think I was crazy? Definitely, but I decided that being happy was more important than being sane. I wanted to be with Cain, and if that meant being his wife, I was okay with it. And he wasn't a complete stranger to me, either. I had been best friends with his cousins for almost a decade and was familiar with his aunt and uncle. Cain was also being open with me, making it easy to trust him.

When it was finally time to go home, I felt a wave of relief. It was stressful having so many eyes on me all at once, but I was going to have to get used to it. As a billionaire's future wife, I wasn't going to be able to hide in the shadows. It was like marrying into a royal family, except with a lot fewer rules.

As I did my hair and makeup in my bathroom, Cain leaned against the door watching me. It was much harder to focus on getting ready when his eyes never left my body.

"You know, if you left the room, I could get this done much faster," I said.

"I'm technically in the doorway, love," Cain replied.

I rolled my eyes. "Hilarious."

He smirked. "I'm glad you appreciate my sense of humor."

I shook my head. "Tell me about your parents."

Cain shrugged. "They're pretty boring. My

father designs cars, and my mother is a housewife. And, as you already know, I'm an only child. For that reason alone, they are particularly excited to meet you."

"You left out the fact that they're ridiculously wealthy, own three houses, and vacation in Europe every summer," I replied.

Cain threw up his hands. "See, you already know everything."

"What if they don't like me?" I asked.

He shook his head. "They'll love you. My mother has been begging me to bring a girl home for ages."

I raised my eyebrows. "Is that why…"

Cain rolled his eyes. "No, love, that's not why I'm marrying you. As much as I adore my mother, she learned a long time ago that she can't compel me to do anything against my will. If I didn't want to marry or if I wanted to be with a circus clown, she couldn't stop me. I believe she was beginning to fear I would be an eternal bachelor. So, when she sees that you are a real, living, breathing woman, she'll be thrilled."

I smiled at him. "I'll do my best not to disappoint."

Cain walked over, wrapped his arms around my waist, and pressed a kiss to the back of my head. "Don't worry, as long as you're not secretly a serial killer or an assassin sent to murder me, they'll like you."

"Do you guys talk about the fact that you're adopted?" I asked.

"It doesn't typically come up in conversation," he replied.

I nodded. "Okay, good to know."

"Why?" he asked. "Were you going to bring it up?"

I met his eyes in the mirror. "No, but I want to know everything about you, Cain. That includes the secrets from those early years of your life that you might not want to tell."

"To be honest, Brea, I don't remember much," he replied. "My brain has blocked most of those memories out, and I'm not sorry about it."

"But the nightmares," I whispered, "they're still happening, right?"

"Yes," he replied.

"Maybe talking about it would help," I said.

"Possibly," he answered, placing a kiss on my neck, "but not tonight."

I knew Cain wanted the conversation to be over, so I let it drop. After I finished getting ready, we left for his childhood home. During the whole car ride, the only thing I could think about was the ring on my finger. Never in my wildest dreams would I have imagined getting engaged to a man I just met. But when I thought about it, it did make a bit of sense. In fact, the idea of an arranged marriage had even appealed to me in the past.

I had always been more serious than other people my own age, always more determined to work instead of play. Much to Mila's displeasure, I had never attended a wild party or gotten drunk at a rave. I was, by most people's standards, completely boring. But it had never bothered me, because I had always known the best years of my life were yet to come. In high school, I hadn't been concerned about becoming prom queen or dating a football player. Instead, I had looked ahead to my future and dreamed of the day I would be able to open my preschool, find love, and have a family of my own. Those had always been my priorities. And like Cain, I had never been a patient person. When I wanted to accomplish something, I didn't let anything get in my way. The same seemed to apply to my new relationship with the man I truly believed would be the love of my life. I'd even met with a matchmaker out of curiosity, but nothing had come of it. Now I could see that it was for the best.

When Wolf pulled the car up in front of Cain's childhood home, my nerves seemed to come to life. Although he had assured me that his parents would like me, I was still apprehensive. What would they think of their son deciding to marry a woman they just met, especially one like me with no money, power, or influence of my own? I brought nothing to the table, and given my future career, that probably wasn't going to change.

"Don't be nervous, love," Cain whispered.

I smiled. "I'll try."

He placed a soft kiss on the top of my head before helping me out of the car. As we made our way up the stonepath, I couldn't help but admire how cozy it looked. Although the house was not at all small, it gave off the aura of a quiet cottage. There were lovely rose bushes surrounding the house, providing a pop of color in front of the sandstone home. It was not where I had pictured Cain's parents living. I had imagined something…darker, more mysterious. Then again, every member of the Kingston family seemed to have their own style and flair.

Before Cain even had a chance to knock, a short woman with brown hair and a comforting smile opened it. Immediately, she stepped forward and wrapped me in her arms. I looked at Cain, uncertain how to react, but he just shrugged.

"Oh, Brea, it is so nice to meet you!" she said.

Cain looked at his mother with a slightly less grumpy expression than was typically on his face. "Brea, this is my mother, Sandy. Mother, this is my future wife, Brea."

Sandy stepped away, taking a moment to look me up and down. "You are absolutely beautiful. Cain was right about you. You're perfect."

I blushed, more than a little relieved. "Thank you."

She took my hand, leading me into the house. "Come right this way, dinner is already on the table. My husband will be so happy to meet you."

Cain followed behind us, allowing his mother to lead the way. When I glanced back at him, he gave me a soft, reassuring smile. Apparently, he wasn't nearly as assertive around his parents. Although that was probably normal, seeing him be so passive was a bit startling. Cain never let himself be led by anyone, except by his mother, it seemed.

Sandy led me into a room with beautiful oak floors, beige-colored walls, and an incredibly high ceiling. In the center of the room was a grand dining table that looked as if it belonged in a palace. Although there were twenty chairs around the table, only four places, two on each side, were set. An older man, whom I assumed was Cain's father, sat on the far side. He had a tight smile on his face, causing my anxiety to spike. Cain didn't even seem to notice. Sandy went to sit beside her husband, and Cain pulled out chairs for him and me.

His father's gaze transferred from me to Cain, allowing me to relax just a little. The two men met each other's eyes, and the room instantly became chilly. What had I missed? Sandy seemed entirely oblivious, clearly just happy to see her son.

I examined the food before me: lobster tails, green beans, and orzo. It was a very sophisticated meal, not exactly the type my parents would have served. Cain hadn't yet commented on the fact that I hadn't told him about my family. Whether it was because he wasn't interested or because he didn't want to pry, I had no idea. I wasn't close to my parents. They seemed far too preoccupied with their own lives to worry much about mine now that I was an adult. They'd never treated me badly, but they hadn't been warm and fuzzy either. My dad was aloof and independent. He'd always pressured me to take care of myself and not rely on anyone. And my mom, well, she was unique. I sometimes worried she would decide to run away to some third-world country and start life over again as a spiritual guru. And if that was what she wanted to do, no one would be able to stop her. Sure, they would be happy for me when I told them I was getting married, but they wouldn't exactly want to help with wedding planning or anything like that.

It seemed like everyone at the table was waiting for someone else to speak first. I glanced at Cain, hoping he would say something to break the icy silence, but he was locked in some kind of silent battle with his father. The two men, both eerily intimidating, glared at each other. I couldn't tell if it was always like this, or if there was something particular they were arguing about. Either way, it caused me to shiver. I never wanted to be on the receiving end of that icy glare. Thankfully, Cain hadn't used it on me yet.

"Father, this is Brea…my future wife," Cain said.

His father glanced at me for only a moment before turning back to Cain. "Are you ready to discuss this yet, or do you plan to continue on foolishly in this delusion? You've made stupid decisions before, but none as consequential as this."

My eyes grew wide. This was certainly not how I'd planned for this dinner to go. I had been worried about making his parents upset with me, but I'd never considered that they might be furious with him. There wasn't exactly anything I could do to remedy the situation either, so I remained silent. I suddenly wished that I could be literally anywhere else.

Sandy looked embarrassed. "Please, Philip, now is not the time. This is our opportunity to get to know Brea and welcome her to the family. She doesn't need to witness this."

Philip ignored his wife and continued glaring at his son. "Well?"

Cain's stare turned murderous. "This is my choice, and I've made it. I'm not a child, Father. I can handle myself."

Philip leaned forward. "I am only trying to protect you. It's your future I'm worried about. I will not stand by and watch you lose everything you've worked for simply because a girl has caught your eye."

I froze. Not only were they clearly in a heated argument, but the topic of discussion was me. I didn't want to cause conflict between him and his parents. They were obviously important to him, or he wouldn't have brought me here in the first place.

"I will not now, or ever, sign a prenup. Do you understand that?" Cain growled.

My eyes grew wide as I watched his father's expression become even more angry. All I wanted to do was blend into my chair and escape this entire situation. I'd never hoped to instantly become invisible more in my entire life.

"We do not need to argue about this in front of Brea," Sandy whispered.

Cain's father shook his head. "On the contrary, I think it's the perfect time."

"There's nothing to discuss," Cain said in a tone that I was surprised didn't send icicles shooting across the room. "Brea is going to be my wife. She will not be barred from my assets. I do not intend to treat her like a child by giving her an allowance. This is not your choice to make, and I am not going to change my mind."

"I don't care if you marry her," Philip replied. "I just want you to protect yourself."

Cain rolled his eyes. "Trust me, father. Brea could be holding a knife to my throat, and there would still be a higher chance that she'd stab herself rather than spill a drop of my blood. She doesn't have a bad bone in her body."

"You might think that now, but wait five years when she has one child on her hip and one in her belly, and she decides to leave you," he whispered. "You will lose everything."

Cain leaned forward, something sinister in his eyes. "And if that were to ever happen, I would rather become destitute than deprive the mother of my children of a single penny. But listen to me when I say that Brea will not ever walk away from me, not if I have anything to say about it. I would never do anything that would make her want to spend a moment away from me, no less leave our marriage."

I looked between the two men. "Um, I'll sign whatever papers I need to. If that's what it takes to make you trust me, Mr. Kingston, then I have no problems doing so."

"No!" Cain shouted, slamming his fist on the table. "I will not allow that."

Philip scoffed. "You're being absurd. Let her do it now while she's still agreeable. There's nothing bad that will come of it. All it does is keep you safe."

Cain looked at me, his eyes staring into my soul. "There is, in fact, a problem with it, Father. It implies that I would ever allow my wife to break her vows and leave my side. If that were to ever happen, it wouldn't matter how much she took because I would have already lost everything."

Sandy looked as if she were about to cry. "Please, Philip. Cain is an adult, and he has clearly made his decision. There's no point in fighting about it. The only thing you're doing is making Brea think we are a terrible family to be part of."

Philip looked at his wife, love filling his eyes. "I'm sorry, Sandy. I know you worked hard preparing this meal, and I don't want to ruin it." His gaze shifted to Cain. "We will let the matter rest, but let it be known that if the worst happens, the responsibility falls on you."

Cain nodded. "Understood."

Sandy smiled at me. "Now, Brea, tell us all about yourself."

Chapter Seventeen

QUESTIONS

Brea

When we were back in the car, Cain finally relaxed. He seemed ready to let the discussion of a prenup rest. I, on the other hand, was not. Truly, everything had happened so fast that the thought of a prenup hadn't even crossed my mind. Since Cain had made me sign an NDA, I had just assumed that he would want to protect himself in other ways, too. He was a billionaire, so it made perfect sense for him to take steps to make sure his financial situation wasn't changed if a divorce ever were to occur. That wasn't what was bothering me, though.

"Cain, what did you mean in there when you said you'd never let me leave?" I whispered.

He looked at me, a frown on his face. "I thought it was clear."

I shook my head. "No, it sounded like you planned on locking me up and never letting me step foot outside the house if I ever thought about leaving you."

Cain sighed. "No, Brea. If you ever truly decided that I wasn't what you wanted, I wouldn't physically or financially prevent you from leaving. In fact, I would do everything in my power to continue to maintain the type of lifestyle you will inevitably become accustomed to. No matter what happens, after our vows are made, I will always view you as my wife. You will be mine. In fact, you already are. If you recall, you've already agreed. That won't change, even if you decide to move to the other side of the world and never speak to me again. However, I am completely confident that I am the right man for you and that you were made to be mine. I will be the type of husband you need and desire. You will never have any reason to doubt my loyalty to you. Therefore, you will not leave."

I bit my lip. "I think your father really is just trying to protect you. The last thing I want is to cause a conflict, especially when it's just over signing a couple of papers."

"It angers me that my father doubts my ability to satisfy your wants and needs," he replied. "No prenup will be signed, and this is the last time we will speak of it."

"I don't think it's about you," I whispered. "I think he just doesn't trust me. Honestly, he has no reason to believe I'm not out for your money. This situation has escalated rather quickly, so it makes sense that he's hesitant ."

Cain's eyes grew even darker. "And that makes me furious. To think that anyone, particularly my father, would view you as anything less than the sweet and innocent woman you are is preposterous. I won't tolerate it."

I reached out to take his hand in mine. "It doesn't bother me."

"Enough, Brea," Cain whispered. "I told you that we are done discussing this, and I do not like repeating myself."

This was a battle I was certainly going to lose, so I decided to give it up. Cain's sincerity and determination to make me happy made me feel all warm and fuzzy inside. He was absolutely certain that he would be a good enough husband that I would never want anyone else. Honestly, I believed it too. It was already clear to me that Cain was not the type of man who spoke words he didn't mean. He would never make a promise, especially marriage vows, that he didn't intend to keep. That meant a lot to me. Like Cain, I took marriage extremely seriously. No one ever planned on getting divorced, but I was especially opposed to it. Although it was hard to admit, I knew that my heart was fragile. I wasn't the type of person who could easily roll with the punches and move on quickly. In fact, I fervently believed that if I ever did get divorced, my heart wouldn't recover, and I would never remarry. It seemed somewhat of a curse to be the type of person who became attached so easily, but could never seem to unstick myself when necessary. I didn't blame others who chose to walk away from marriages and start over, especially toxic or abusive ones; it just wasn't for me. I didn't have that kind of strength.

"I need you in my office tomorrow at noon," Cain said.

"That's fine, but why?" I asked.

He sighed. "We're going to be doing an exclusive interview with a newspaper. Unfortunately, reporters are always trying to get some sort of news about my personal life. Apparently, people just love keeping up with the rich and famous. It's incredibly annoying, and I'm sorry to subject you to it. I promise, once the wedding is past and we settle into normal life, I will shield you from them as much as possible. But so far, what I've learned is that the best way to prevent reporters from following you everywhere you go is to just give them an interview. That way they're satisfied."

"What are they going to ask?" I replied.

"They've already given me the list of questions," he said, handing me a small piece of paper. His eyes looked apologetic.

I examined the list, reading the questions one by one:

1.Given that the two of you have known each other for such a short period of time, what made you decide to become engaged so quickly?

2. Does your age difference pose any potential problems?

3. What will the life of Mrs. Cain Kingston look like?

4. When should we expect wedding bells?

5.Do you plan on having children?

6.Finally, is there anything else you'd like to tell us?

"This is crazy," I said.

"Those were the less invasive questions," Cain whispered. "They sent over two drafts before this, and I trashed them both. Don't worry, I'll answer them. You just have to sit there and smile. I promise, it'll be fine."

I frowned. "I don't like this, Cain. Why should everyone who decides to pick up this paper get to know all about our plans for the future? We haven't even discussed what type of wedding we'll have or when it will take place."

He leaned down and placed a soft kiss on my forehead. "The answers will be short and cryptic, love. I've done interviews before. They won't get any information out of me that I don't want them to know. It will be over quickly, and you won't have to worry about it again."

"I'm placing my trust in you," I whispered. "Please, Cain, don't let them swarm me like a pack of hyenas out for blood."

He took my face in his hands, looking directly into my eyes. "Don't worry that pretty little brain of yours, love. I will take care of everything."

I closed my eyes as he tilted his head up to kiss me, letting his lips pull me into a blissful peace.

Chapter Eighteen

PURE

Brea

I had never been so fidgety in my entire life. Cain and I were sitting beside each other in his office, waiting for the reporter to arrive. He was already irritated because she was ten minutes late. I, on the other hand, hoped she never showed up.

Cain wore one of his signature black suits with his hair nicely groomed and a look of dominance in his eyes. For my entire life, I had questioned the existence of alpha males. The whole concept seemed made up and like a good excuse for certain men to be able to do whatever they wanted and blame it on biology. But after meeting Cain, my perspective had been completely changed. There was no doubt in my mind that, whatever time period or civilization he had been born into, he would have made his way to the top of the food chain. He commanded respect everywhere he went. Women fawned over him, and other men did their best to get on his good side. I was drawn to him on some raw, primal level that wasn't explainable by the modern views on love and attraction. And though the feminist side of my brain struggled and fought against it, the part of me that desperately wanted him easily won.

I sat pressed up against him, gripping his arm like his touch was the difference between life and death. Wearing a loose, feminine dress and plain ballerina flats with my hair falling down around me in waves, I certainly knew I looked beautiful. That wasn't the point, though. I was worried about being caught off guard by this reporter, terrified that I would say something I'd regret. I didn't want to appear weak or foolish.

Just as I was about to beg Cain to call the whole interview off, the door to his office opened. A short woman in a tight black pantsuit entered the room. She had a bright blue bob, bold makeup, and a hint of mischief on her face. Cain held the same look of annoyance he had before she'd entered, but unlike most people, the woman didn't seem startled by it.

"You're late," Cain said with a look that could kill.

The woman nodded. "My apologies, Mr. Kingston. Your security took a bit longer to get through than I had anticipated."

A hint of amusement crossed Cain's face. "Well, we had to make sure all of the conditions were met."

"Yes," she replied, "no cameras or recording

devices. You made that extremely clear in your email."

Relief washed over me. Perhaps this wouldn't be as bad as I expected. He had taken precautions.

"Sit, and let's get this over with," Cain commanded.

The woman raised her eyebrows, clearly not happy with his tone. "I will try not to take more of your time than necessary, Mr. Kingston."

He nodded, motioning to the chair across from us. She sat down before pulling out a pen and a notepad. I still clung to Cain's arm, hoping that I might just disappear and leave him to deal with her alone. This must have been what fish felt like before they were devoured by a shark.

The woman's gaze turned to me. "My name is River Young. I'll be conducting your interview today. I believe you both already know most of the topics we're going to cover. Before we begin, do you have any questions for me?"

I looked at Cain, shaking my head. "No, I don't believe so."

River nodded. "Great, we'll move along then. So, given that the two of you have known each other for such a short period of time, what made you decide to become engaged so quickly?"

Cain placed his hand on my thigh, gently running his thumb across my skin. "Many people have said that when you find the one, it's clear right from the start. I couldn't agree more. My own parents married just two months after meeting, so the idea of a quick and short engagement has never been strange to me. When I saw Brea, I knew I wanted to marry her."

River looked to me. "And you, Ms. Paige?"

I squeezed Cain's arm even harder. "Like Mr. Kingston said, we were attracted to each other the moment we met. I've dreamed of getting married for so long, and now that I've found the perfect man, there doesn't seem to be any reason to wait."

River looked displeased by my answer. It was clear that she was fishing for some kind of secret, but I couldn't tell what it was. There truly wasn't any sort of great conspiracy going on. What I had told her was the truth.

"Alright," she replied. "Does your age difference pose any potential problems?"

Cain shook his head. "Not at all. Ms. Paige and I are both consenting adults with similar hopes and ambitions. We also share a love for philanthropy, and plan to make charitable work a large part of our lives."

River glanced at me. "Ms. Paige, do you have any comments?"

All I wanted to do was run out of the room as quickly as possible, but I managed to steady my voice. "I have the same view as my fiancé. Our age difference has no impact on our relationship. I care about who Mr. Kingston is as a person, not what year he was born."

"How sweet," River replied, but her tone did not convey the same sentiment. "So, what will the life of Mrs. Cain Kingston look like?"

Cain looked down at me, smiling. "Ms. Paige has always dreamed of opening a preschool for disadvantaged children. After she finishes her education, that is what she intends to pursue. I fully support her goal and intend to help her in whatever way I can."

"Is there anything else?" River asked.

I gave her a sweet, but very fake, smile. "Mr. Kingston is correct. I do intend to open a preschool. Apart from that, and completing my degree, I simply intend to be a good wife and partner. That's the most important thing."

"Lovely," River grumbled.

Cain raised his eyebrows. "Is there a problem?"

River's expression immediately turned to one of professionalism. "No, of course not. Now, moving on to something everyone is curious about, when should we expect wedding bells?"

I looked up at Cain. We hadn't talked about how we were going to address this question. And truthfully, I didn't have a good answer. I had meant to bring it up last night, but I'd forgotten.

"Next week," Cain replied. "Patience is not one of my virtues."

My eyes just about popped out of my head.

How exactly did he plan on organizing a wedding so quickly? I didn't have a dress or anything else. Was he even thinking about those details? Just go with the flow, a little voice in my head whispered. I kept my mouth shut with a smile plastered on my face. Cain hadn't been kidding when he'd said he was bad at waiting.

A look of surprise crossed River's face. "So soon? Congratulations. I'm sure you have a lot to do before the ceremony. Since you're in such a rush to marry, I have to ask: Do you plan on having children anytime soon? "

Cain nodded. "Although Ms. Paige and I would like to keep the details private, I will confirm that we would like to have a sizable family."

River's gaze drifted toward me. "Ms. Paige, any comments?"

"Like Mr. Kingston said, that is something we'd like to keep between ourselves until a later date. I'm sure that when the time comes, we'll make an announcement," I answered.

River quickly scribbled something down on her notepad before looking at Cain with a renewed sense of confidence. "Just one more question, Mr. Kingston. It's been widely known that you have been a bachelor for many years, rejecting countless accomplished women with impressive careers and backgrounds. The question everyone is wondering, but is too afraid to ask, is: does Ms. Paige's youth and likely purity have anything to do with your choice to marry her rather than a more established woman with a life of her own?"

My jaw dropped so far I thought it might hit the floor. That question had certainly not been on the list. My body was entirely frozen, and though I wanted to scream at her to leave, my mouth couldn't seem to move. Cain looked like a bomb about to go off, but to my surprise, he was actually holding himself together better than I was.

"Tread very carefully," he whispered.

River cleared her throat. "What I'm trying to ask is, have there been any examinations done on Ms. Paige similar to those rumored to have been conducted on the late Princess Diana before her marriage? After all, Mr. Kingston, many people view you as a king in your own right. And, given your rejection of countless other more mature, established women, everyone is wondering what the qualifications were for Ms. Paige to become your fiancée."

Cain practically jumped out of his seat. For a moment, I worried he might march over to River and strangle her to death. My heart was beating so fast that I could barely hear myself think, and it was all I could do to focus on breathing. What right did she think she had to ask such a personal and outrageous question? If Cain had known about it, he never would have let her in here. Was that really what people thought, that he had picked me because I was…pure?

"Get out of my office!" Cain growled.

A look of satisfaction crossed River's face. "Of course, Mr. Kingston, I apologize for upsetting you."

"If I ever see your face again, you will regret it," he whispered.

River scrambled out of her seat, finally seeming to understand just how dangerous my future husband could be. Without another glance in my direction, she hurriedly left the office and disappeared from sight.

Cain leaned down, wiping a tear off my cheek. Before he did so, I hadn't even realized I was crying. His eyes held a level of fury I'd never seen before.

"Brea," he whispered, "I am so sorry."

It was all I could do to stop myself from curling up into a ball and sobbing.

"Wolf!" Cain shouted.

Within moments, Wolf burst into the room. He looked ready to kill any intruder who had somehow made it inside Cain's heavily secured office. The moment Wolf's eyes landed on me, his gaze softened silently. Then, his expression turned to one of anger.

"What happened?" he asked. "Are you hurt, ma'am ?"

"I need you to take her home now," Cain replied. "Make sure you use the back door so no one sees you, and get Bianca to bring her whatever she needs as soon as she's back in her room." Cain looked down at me. "I'll be there as soon as I can, love. But in order to prevent myself from running after that woman and making her regret ever setting foot in this building, I need to make some phone calls."

"What—what are you going to do?" I asked.

He tucked a stray piece of hair behind my ear. "I'm going to make sure she never works in the industry again, Brea. Believe me when I say that the only job she will ever get after this will keep her as far away from you as possible."

"Is that really what everyone thinks about me?" I whispered. "That-that you picked me because I'm young and pure?"

He pulled me into his arms, squeezing me so tightly I almost couldn't breathe. "No, love. She was just trying to get a reaction out of me, and she succeeded. But I will make her regret it, I promise you that."

Cain stepped away. "Wolf, take her home. And if anyone follows you, I honestly don't care what you do to them. Whatever it is can be fixed by signing a check. Just make sure she gets home safely, and I will be there as soon as I can."

Wolf nodded. "Yes, sir. Ms. Paige, please come with me."

I grabbed Cain's arm, and a look of pain crossed his face. "Brea, if you don't go with Wolf now, you will see a side of me that I'd rather you didn't. Please go with him voluntarily, or I will have him pick you up and carry you out of here."

I looked at Wolf, but he shook his head. "Ma'am, I don't want to drag you out the door, but if you don't come with me in the next five seconds, I will."

"Fine," I grumbled.

Cain nodded. "Thank you, love. Wolf, take her now."

Wolf lightly placed his hand on my arm, leading me out of the office. When I glanced back for one last look at Cain, I saw an expression on his face that made my blood run cold.

Chapter Nineteen

REVENGE

Cain

I let out a sigh of relief as soon as Wolf removed Brea from my office. The last thing I needed was for her to see me with my anger at its height. Had the reporter in my office been a man, I would have taken him down just as quickly as I had Charles. I didn't believe in hitting women, though, no matter what awful things they said. But when I had witnessed the pain in Brea's eyes, I had wanted to knock River unconscious. No one was allowed to make my woman unhappy without facing the consequences. It was unacceptable. And although I would not retaliate physically, she would still suffer.

I picked up my phone, immediately entering the number for the owner of the newspaper River worked for. Brian and I had known each other for years, and given that I had provided him with several exclusive interviews, he always wanted to keep me happy.

As expected, Brian answered the phone quickly. "Cain, nice to hear from you. How did the interview go?"

It was a challenge to keep my voice steady. "If you don't fire that woman in the next hour, your newspaper will never have another interview with me or any of my associates again."

Brian paused. "What happened?"

It took everything I had not to shout at him. "She implied some incredibly inappropriate things about my relationship with Brea, including suggesting that I had ordered some sort of physical purity exam on her. Your reporter also made it extremely clear that she believed I'm only marrying Brea for her…innocence."

"Oh no," Brian replied, "I am so sorry, Cain. I can't express how sorry I am. Don't worry, your request will be met. Her office will be cleaned out today, and I'll put a word out to others in the industry that she is unprofessional and shouldn't be trusted."

"Good," I replied, ending the call.

A knock sounded on my door. "Mr. Kingston, someone is here to see you."

I closed my eyes. The last thing I wanted to do was stay in the building and discuss business. I needed to be home with Brea, making sure that she wasn't having a complete breakdown. What if she believed even a sliver of what that reporter had implied about our relationship? But I had a job to do, and I couldn't abandon my responsibilities. Brea was home safe, and Bianca would take care of her. That would have to do until I could make it back.

"Send them in, Olive," I replied.

I turned around, leaning back against my desk. But when I saw who entered the door, I felt a genuine sense of surprise. This was certainly not who I had expected my visitor to be."

"You," Charles said, holding up the newspaper detailing his crimes on the front of it, "you did this to me. I won't let you get away with it."

I raised my eyebrows. "You must be mistaken, Charles. I'm not in the habit of writing or publishing celebrity gossip. Your financial situation is of no interest to me."

Charles shook his head. "Don't play dumb, Kingston. You arranged this because I touched your little pet, isn't that right?"

"Do not even speak of my fiancée again, do you understand me?" I whispered.

He let out a drunken laugh. "Your fiancée? Is this some kind of joke? She's nobody! What's her biggest accomplishment? A good GPA? She's just a toy you'll get tired of."

Although I had vowed not to be violent today, I was unable to stop my fist from colliding with his face. Charles fell backward, a surprised look on his face. What exactly had he thought was going to happen? It was clear that he was drunk, but I had no clue that being intoxicated would make him so incredibly stupid.

Charles attempted to stand up, but fell back

down before he could get his footing. There was blood all over his face and my fist. For a moment, I considered shoving him out my office door and locking it behind him. Olive could call security to come remove him. But when he threw the newspaper at me, I lost the rest of my self-control.

I reached down, punching him over and over until my fists were shaking. Shockingly, Charles was still conscious when I pulled away. His face was a bloody mess, though, and so was my shirt. If Brea saw me like this, she would probably be terrified. She was too good, too…sweet to witness such violence.

Charles looked at me as if I were a monster, and maybe he was right. But I didn't care what he, or anyone for that matter, thought about me. The only person whose opinion mattered was Brea. If she saw me as anything other than her lover and protector, I would never recover. Since the moment she'd walked into my office, I'd been enchanted. She wasn't simply a drug that I craved. No, Brea was the oxygen I needed to survive. And I would never let anything or anyone get in the way of her being mine for as long as I lived.

"What is wrong with you?" Charles asked, fear in his voice.

"I should ask you that," I replied. "You cheat on your wife, provide for a mistress, father a secret child, and get accused of all manner of despicable things, then have the nerve to come in here and be angry about what I did to protect my woman. You have no right to think, no less speak of, her again. Is that understood?"

For the briefest moment, I thought he might try to attempt a verbal attack. Charles clearly thought better of it, though. This was the second time I had knocked him to the floor without breaking a sweat. Continuing to anger me further would only cause him more problems.

"My wife is leaving me," he whispered.

"Good," I replied, motioning toward the door. "No woman deserves to be disrespected in the way you do to her. I hope she takes everything from you. The legal system doesn't look kindly upon men who are disloyal to their wives. And in case you hadn't noticed, neither do I. Now, get out."

Charles stumbled to his feet and clumsily made his way to the door. Olive's eyes grew wide when she saw the blood both he and I were covered in, but she didn't say anything. After Charles had stepped onto the elevator, I looked at her.

"Olive, could you please get Wolf back here as quickly as possible to drive me home? Cancel the rest of my meetings for the day," I said.

She nodded, her voice a bit shaky. "Of course, sir. I'll call him."

"Thank you," I replied, walking toward the bathroom to clean the blood off my hands.

Chapter Twenty
WAIT FOR IT

Brea

Much to Wolf and Bianca's displeasure, I had refused to go to my room until Cain returned. Instead, I sat by the front door drinking the cup of tea that Bianca had practically begged me to take. What was it like for Cain to have so much power that he could destroy a person's career without exerting any real effort or energy? If that reporter hadn't been so unprofessional, I would have felt bad about her getting fired. On a small level, I still did. But I didn't want her to treat anyone else the way she had us, so it was probably for the best that her line of work was changed.

When I heard the car pull up outside, I jumped out of my seat and yanked the door open. Cain was… covered in blood. I ran to him as quickly as I could, examining for injuries.

"It's not mine, love," he said.

I reached up to touch his face. "What happened after I left? Did someone try to hurt you? Was it that reporter?"

He shook his head. "Just after you left, Charles stopped by my office."

My jaw dropped. "And he fought you?"

Cain frowned. "Sort of. He said some very… unsavory things about you, and I made my displeasure known by giving him two black eyes and a split lip. Don't worry, he'll be fine. I didn't hurt him that badly; there's just a lot of blood."

I pressed myself against his chest, desperate to feel his arms around me. Cain leaned down, placing a soft kiss on top of my head before gently pushing me away. Pain flickered across my face.

"Let me get changed, Brea," he said. "I don't want that man's blood on you again."

I nodded. "Okay."

He smiled softly. "Thank you, love. How about you change into something more comfortable? I'll have Wolf go pick us up some pizza, and we can watch a movie in the theater. Anything you want."

My spirit lifted. "That actually sounds great."

His eyes sparkled. "Then it's a plan. Go get changed. I'll be up in a minute, just let me talk to Wolf."

I dashed upstairs, finally relieved that he was back home safe and that we were going to watch a movie together. It was such a normal, mundane thing to do. I had actually never thought about how funny it would be to see Cain Kingston in his pajamas eating pizza and popcorn, but the mental image made me giggle. Was this what our life would be like? Maybe sometimes we could pretend to be average people. Although the in-home staff might make that a little bit difficult. As I continued hurrying to my room, I wasn't paying attention to where I was going and accidentally ran straight into Ingrid.

"Hey!" she shouted. "Watch where you're going! Do you have no manners?"

"Oh, I am so sorry," I replied with sincerity. "I was just in a hurry to get out of this dress and..."

She raised her eyebrows. "And what?"

I bit my lip. "And go back downstairs to watch a movie with Cain."

If it were possible for someone to turn green with envy, Ingrid would have done so right then and there. "I see. Well, I hope you enjoy the time you have with him because it will be short. Don't get comfortable."

I suddenly felt emboldened. "We're getting married...next week."

Genuine shock crossed her face. "He'll never go through with it."

I crossed my arms over my chest. "Why's that?"

Ingrid looked me up and down, an expression of disgust on her face. Without another word, she stormed off in the opposite direction, her blond curls bouncing behind her. I rolled my eyes, wondering just how much persuasion it would take to convince Cain to get rid of her. He didn't seem to have any problem making people who were unkind to me suffer. Ingrid certainly checked that box. Yet, he had defended her once before. Why? I pushed that question to the back of my mind, deciding that it wasn't the time to worry about it.

After changing into a matching set of pink joggers and a hoodie, I made my way down to the theater. When I entered the room, I was immediately overwhelmed by the delicious smell of pizza and garlic bread. But when my eyes landed on Cain, I forgot all about the food. He stood wearing a pair of grey sweatpants and a skin-tight t-shirt that put his chest and abdominal muscles on display. I had never seen a more perfectly sculpted man than the one before me. He had clearly taken a shower because his hair was still dripping wet and his skin was practically glowing, somehow making him even more handsome than usual. It was impossible to view him as anything other than breathtakingly attractive. No one, not even the most impartial judge, could have denied his physical superiority. Don't get me wrong, I loved when Cain wore his fancy suits, but something about seeing him like this, all casual and relaxed, made my stomach do backflips. He was like a Greek god in the flesh.

"You look adorable," Cain said, a wide smile on his face.

I blushed. "Well, you don't look too bad either."

He smirked. "Is that so?"

I bit my lip. "Absolutely."

Cain walked over and placed his hands on my hips. The moment he touched me, my senses heightened. He awakened something deep inside my soul, a part of me that I had yet to explore or even discover. I had no idea what it was about him, but this man made me question everything I'd ever thought I believed about love and soul mates. Never before had I accepted the proposal that you could fall in love with someone at first sight. It seemed crazy, even childish. But after meeting Cain, after falling so hard and so fast, I knew it was indeed possible. Love could flow gently like a stream, but it could also hit you like a brick to the face. In my case, the latter had happened. I would have died for this man even though we had known each other for barely any time at all. But what truly made my heart beat faster was that I knew he would burn the world down to keep me safe and not regret it for a single moment. Was that wrong? Maybe. But did it make me even more infatuated with him? For sure.

"I love when you're relaxed around me, when you're comfortable," he whispered.

I looked into his eyes. "Why?"

He brushed a piece of hair out of my face. "Because for just a few moments, it allows me to forget everything about my chaotic life and simply enjoy the sight of a woman who could make kings and emperors fall to their knees with her beauty."

I glanced away, slightly amused. "You're certainly an expert at flattery."

He grabbed my face, tilting my chin up so his lips could meet mine. "It's not flattery, Brea. It's the truth. You have absolutely no idea what you do to me. I would rip my heart out without a moment's hesitation if that was what would make you happy. I lose all sense of reason and logic around you; it's maddening."

"You're crazy," I whispered.

"Crazy for you," he replied.

I reached up, pulling his head down and touching my lips to his. Tangling my hands in his hair, I pushed our bodies closer together. He tasted of coffee beans and warm cinnamon. Cain's lips were so much softer than I would have ever believed them to be before kissing him that first night when I had agreed to be his. His touch was a delicious combination of luxury and danger that only made me fall harder and harder every second our bodies were in contact. Before Cain, I had believed that desire this strong only existed in fairytales, that I would never find the type of love I had dreamed of as a little girl. But now I could truly see that all the romance novels I had ever read weren't simply fictional. No, they described feelings and emotions that were all too real. I pushed Cain against the wall, kissing him with an urgency that seemed to surprise us both.

"Brea," Cain whispered.

I looked into his eyes. "Yes?"

He brushed a piece of hair out of my face. "Not now."

"Why?" I questioned.

He smiled softly. "Because you are special. And although I am not a patient man, I can wait a week to make you mine in every way. I want our wedding night to make your mind explode, and in order for that to happen, I need to keep you in suspense. One week, Brea, and then you will have as much of me as you could possibly want."

"Did I do something wrong?" I whispered.

He shook his head. "No, love . I just want to distinguish you from the women I've been with before. You are more important to me than you could possibly imagine, and I never want you to doubt how precious you are. This connection we have…it's amazing. I honestly never believed I would fall in love, yet here we are. One week, that's all I ask."

"You…love me?" I whispered.

He placed a soft kiss on my forehead. "I fell in love with you the moment you walked into my office, and our eyes met for the first time. That day, I knew I wanted you to be mine no matter what it took."

My eyes began to water. "I love you, too. And I can't wait to be your wife."

A look of pure adoration filled Cain's eyes. "Oh, my love. Just wait. In one week, I will show you just how desperate I am to be your husband."

Chapter Twenty-One

ESCAPE

Cain

In less than twenty-four hours, Brea would belong to me. She would be mine, and no one on this earth or beyond would be able to take her away. Already, if another man so much as looked in her direction, I wanted to kill him. She would likely find that distasteful, though, so I had to control myself, at least around her. But after tomorrow, I would never let her escape. She would be my wife, and I had no intention of ever letting her walk away. I would do everything in my power to make sure she was the happiest, most content woman in the world. She would finish college, start her preschool, and have our babies. No matter what it took, I would ensure that she was never sad or disappointed again. Brea could not even begin to imagine just how much control she had over me, but that was probably for the best. Although I knew that if she did, she wouldn't use it against me. She was too kind and honest to ever manipulate anyone, especially her husband.

When I had heard her profess her love, it felt as if the world stopped spinning. Women had been obsessed with me before, but it was never because of who I was as a person. They always wanted my money, power, and influence. Truthfully, I hadn't blamed them. After all, I desired those things too. The difference was that I was willing to work and dedicate myself to achieving and maintaining them. And so, I had vowed that the woman I chose to be my wife would not be a money-hungry vixen, but a sweet, kind soul that only needed love and affection. Brea was perfect, and I had mentally marked her as mine the moment I saw the honesty and openness in her eyes. The fact that her soft body and perfect lips made me want to explode was just a bonus.

I adjusted my tie and glanced at myself in the mirror. Brea and I would see each other for the last time tonight before she walked down the aisle tomorrow. We were going to one of my favorite restaurants with fabulous French cuisine. I had rented out the entire restaurant and arranged for a string quartet to play her favorite songs. Brea would have the best night of her life, well, until tomorrow anyway.

Stepping out into the hallway, I was met with the sight of a very scantily dressed Ingrid. My eyes grew wide, and a sly smile crossed her face. This was certainly not going to end the way she wanted.

"Ingrid, why exactly are you standing outside my door in a dress that looks as though it's been torn to shreds by a tiger?" I asked.

She bit her lip, twirling one of her blond curls around her fingers. "Mr. Kingston, I was hoping to speak with you."

I raised my eyebrows. "About what? A jungle cat on the loose?"

She took a step toward me. "About tomorrow, sir. You and I both know she won't be able to provide you with what you need. She's too…fragile ."

"Get out of my way, Ingrid," I replied. "I'm late for dinner."

The next thing I knew, her lips were on mine. It only took a moment for me to push her away, but it was too late. I heard a gasp at the end of the hall. Brea was standing there, a look of horror on her face.

I looked at Ingrid. "You knew she was there! This was a setup!"

Ingrid smirked. "Sir, I don't know what you're talking about."

"Brea!" I called.

But when I turned to look for her, she was done. Panic coursed through me.

"You will pay for this, Ingrid," I growled. "If I ever have to see your face again, it will be the worst day of your life. "

Without another word, I took off down the hallway. I ran downstairs, frantically calling Brea's name. To my dismay, she seemed to have disappeared without a trace.

"Wolf!" I shouted.

He was by my side in seconds. "Sir, what's wrong?"

"Where is she?" I asked.

"Who, sir?" he replied.

I frowned. "Brea! Did you see her? Where did she go?"

Embarrassment crossed his face. "I don't know. I didn't realize I was supposed to be watching her. I apologize."

Suddenly, a car engine started outside. We both dashed to the door in time to see the Bentley, one of the many cars in my collection, pull away. I looked at Wolf.

"How did she get the keys?" I growled.

He shook his head. "I have no idea, sir."

"Track her. I don't care if she goes to Timbuktu. We're following her," I said.

"Of course," he replied, running out the door to start what I hoped was the fastest car I owned.

Chapter Twenty-Two

LITTLE LAMB

Brea

As I drove, tears poured down my face. How could he do this to me? How could he give a grand speech about me being special and then kiss her? Ingrid had been right, I wasn't enough for Cain. Had he been secretly having an affair with her this whole time? How long had this been going on? What made it worse was that I had fallen for it. I had been so naive as to believe that Cain Kingston would want a girl like me. Maybe he got mad at that reporter because what she'd said was true. Did he want me as an innocent little trophy wife to tote around at fancy events and have his babies, but give his heart to someone else? How had I been so stupid to agree to marry him? Was I honestly that foolish? Maybe this was the wakeup call I needed to see reality and run for the hills. No reasonable woman married a man she'd just met. That was reserved for children's stories and reality TV.

I had absolutely no clue where I was going to go. If I went anywhere familiar, Cain would find me. He was probably already trying to track my movements. Luckily, this car was fast. On the downside, I had no idea how to drive it. I had just grabbed the first set of keys I saw and rushed out of there as quickly as I could. I had no intention of ever going back. Evan and Enzo had been right; Cain wasn't the one for me. I could never be what he needed.

After about an hour of driving way over the speed limit, I came across a small diner that looked like it had been around for at least a century. That was when I realized I didn't have any money. I screamed, banging my hands against the steering wheel. Then, my eyes landed on the wad of hundred-dollar bills sitting on the console. Of course, having hundreds of dollars sitting around in each one of his cars seemed like something a billionaire would do. He was careless with his money, just like he was with my heart. All of it was replaceable to him.

My hands were shaking as I picked up the cash and exited the car. I was fully aware that I looked entirely out of place. On Cain's insistence, I was wearing a long, black silk dress and designer stilettos for what was supposed to be a fancy dinner the night before our wedding. He had promised me a lovely time with delicious food and a romantic atmosphere, but now all of that was ruined. And because of him, I was now in the middle of nowhere, dressed like I was about to walk down the red carpet. That was hardly my biggest problem, though.

When I walked into the diner, everyone stopped talking as they all gawked at my appearance. I wanted to just curl up in a ball and die, but I was absolutely starving. Maybe I could call someone to come get me. Mila would certainly come to my rescue and not say a word to anyone else if I asked. But when I looked down at my phone, I realized it was dead. *Great,* I thought. *This day was going from bad to worse.*

"Um, can I help you, ma'am?" a girl about my age asked.

She had a long ponytail with a nervous expression on her face.

"Yes, uh, could I have a sandwich or something?" I asked.

She nodded. "Sure, would you like to sit down?"

"Yes, thank you," I replied, mindlessly following her to an empty table.

"I'll be right back," she said.

I closed my eyes, attempting to ignore all the sultry stares from the men in the room. I tried to stop myself from crying, but the tears continued to drip down my face. How was it possible to cry for so long without melting into pieces?

"Hey there, pretty thing," a deep voice said.

A man with a scruffy beard, dirty boots, and a cowboy hat stood in front of me. He had a look on his face that made me want to throw up, but I managed to contain my disgust. The man leaned forward, his eyes traveling down to graze over my chest.

"What are you doing here alone? Did somebody break your heart?" he asked.

I frowned at him. "None of your business, please leave me alone."

He grinned. "I specialize in broken hearts, sweetie. How about you come with me for the night? I promise I'll make you feel better than the loser who has you crying."

"I highly doubt that," Cain said, making me jump. "Now, please step away. I'm here to collect my runaway bride. She seems to have wandered a bit far from home."

All eyes in the room turned to him. Cain towered over the other man. He looked even more out of place here than I did. Cain glanced down at me, a look of fury in his eyes.

"I need to take her back to where she belongs," he whispered, his tone clipped and serious. "The little lamb has escaped her pasture, but not for long."

The other man, clearly intimidated by Cain, stepped away. I was frozen still, unable to think or move. Part of me was glad that Cain had arrived to rescue me from this mob of men with less than pleasant intentions. But at the same time, he was the reason I was here in the first place. Cain had betrayed my trust and shattered my heart into a million pieces. What made him think that I even wanted to see him again?

"How did you find me?" I asked.

Cain sat down, clearly displeased at my choice of restaurant. "You took one of my cars, Brea. It has a GPS tracker. You're not exactly a master thief. I'd recommend you never try to become a fugitive. It won't end well."

"Why are you here?" I asked.

He frowned. "That's a ridiculous question. I came to take you home."

"My home isn't with you," I whispered. "Not anymore."

He leaned forward. "Your home will always be with me, Brea. I know what I said before about not locking you up, but I've changed my mind. If I have to carry you out of here kicking and screaming, I will. Then I'll bolt all the doors and windows shut until you come back to your senses." His eyes softened. "I won't lose you, I can't."

The man was talking like a crazy person. How could he expect me to marry him when everything he'd said to me had been a lie? I deserved better than that.

"You-you kissed her," I sobbed.

He sobbed. "On the contrary, she kissed me. You have my word, it was very much against my will. And she will suffer because of it. Neither of us will ever have to see her again. She's gone, and I will make sure she never gains employment on this side of the country again. Ending people's careers seems to be my new hobby. I don't enjoy it, but I will always do everything within my power to protect you."

Was he telling the truth? I had no way of knowing. What if this was all just an act to convince me to go back and be his good little wife? I wanted to believe him, though. Perhaps I had to give him the benefit of the doubt. After all, his story made sense. It had been clear to me since the beginning that Ingrid was not to be trusted. I had known she would do something crazy, but I hadn't expected this. Still, it was hard to just accept everything he was saying and move on without asking any questions.

"Why did you keep her around in the first place?" I whispered.

His eyes met mine. "She comes from the same world as me, Brea. So does Wolf. I try to give people who didn't have a great start in life a chance. If someone is willing to work hard and do their best, I believe they should be given the opportunity to move up in the world. When Ingrid came to me, she was like that. Over the years, she obviously changed."

"Were you ever…involved with her?" I asked.

He shook his head. "No, never. She's not my type. I knew she was attracted to me, but I thought it was a passing infatuation. I had no idea she would actually try something. If I had suspected that, I would have fired her much sooner."

The waitress walked up to the table with a sandwich in hand. "Here you go, miss. Can I get you something to eat, sir?"

Cain's eyes never left mine. "There is no way you're eating that."

I frowned. "Why? I'm hungry."

Cain glared at me. "This place has more health code violations than I can count. There's a dead mouse over there in the corner, Brea. I'd prefer you didn't get food poisoning the night before our wedding."

The girl's face turned red in embarrassment. "Oh, sir. I'm so sorry you had to see that. I'll get someone to clean it up right away."

Cain handed her a fifty-dollar bill. "You can go now."

Without hesitation, she took the money and hurried away.

"We are leaving, now," Cain said, standing up from the table. "And if you try to pick up that sandwich, I will snatch it out of your hand."

Once again, everyone was staring at us, and my face turned bright red. "Okay, okay, let's go. Don't make a scene."

Cain grabbed my arm. "Oh, love, trust me. If you ever try to run from me again, I will cause a much bigger stir than startling a few people in a diner. You haven't seen anything yet. Don't make me do this again."

I nodded, hurrying to keep up with him as he stormed out the door. When we made it outside, I saw Wolf standing by the Porsche.

"Wolf, take the Bentley. I'll drive Brea back. She's not leaving my sight again," Cain said. "Brea, get in the car."

Wolf handed Cain the keys to the Porsche and walked away. He was definitely not happy with me. Honestly, I could understand why. Storming off might not have been the most mature thing to do, but it had seemed like a good idea at the time.

"I think Wolf might be upset," I said.

Cain rolled his eyes. "Oh, really? Get in the car."

I frowned, crossing my arms over my chest.

Cain closed his eyes. "Please."

"Fine," I grumbled.

When Cain was seated in the car, he looked over at me. "You are never, ever picking where we eat. That place is revolting."

"I was hungry," I replied. "And it was the first place I saw that was open. Besides, I didn't think you'd find me there."

He frowned. "How stupid do you think I am?"

"I'm sorry," I whispered.

Cain pulled the car out onto the road and began driving. "I am too, Brea. I promised never to hurt you, and I failed. You have no idea how much I hate myself right now for even causing you the tiniest bit of pain.

It's…excruciating."

"I just panicked," I whispered. "I assumed the worst, and that wasn't fair. You're right to be angry with me. It's not your fault that she kissed you. You've never done anything else to break my trust. Everything has happened so quickly that I have a lot of heightened emotions. Maybe I'm not thinking clearly."

A look of relief washed over Cain's face. In hindsight, I shouldn't have run away like a child. But I was already so terrified that I was undeserving of him, and seeing him with Ingrid had made me panic. If Cain didn't care about us, he wouldn't be working so hard to protect me. And if he was going to be unfaithful and jeopardize our marriage, it was unlikely that he'd be so opposed to a prenup. Cain had made it clear that I was special to him. Although he had given the appearance of being angry at me in the diner, I could tell by the look on his face that he was actually furious with himself. When he said he wanted to make me happy, he meant it. Honestly, I had a feeling that he was even more insecure than I was.

"I hope you can forgive me," Cain said, regret in his voice.

I smiled at him. "There's nothing to forgive. I'm sorry for not trusting you."

It almost looked as if he might cry. "I'll never give you reason to doubt me again, I promise. You have my undying devotion, Brea. From now until forever. You are mine, and I am yours. That's the way fate destined it to be."

"I will love you forever," I whispered.

He brought my hand up to his lips and softly kissed it. "Thank you, love. Thank you."

Chapter Twenty-Three
WEDDING BELLS

Brea

The wedding went off without a hitch. To my surprise, Cain hadn't wanted a big ceremony. The only guests were family members and a few close friends. As expected, Mila was sobbing the entire time with mascara and eyeliner running down her face. Evan and Enzo, despite their initial hesitations, truly seemed happy for me. Of course, they had made Cain swear that he would never break my heart. After a serious conversation with threats of killing him if he hurt me, Evan and Enzo had finally given their approval. Of course, Cain didn't care if they were okay with it or not, but he knew I did, so he listened to their lecture and made a million promises about treating me well.

My favorite part of the ceremony had been our first dance. The entire time, Cain stared into my eyes with a look that spoke more than a thousand words. The way his gaze traveled across my body and over my sheath wedding dress made my heart pound so fast I was sure everyone for miles around could hear it. It was hard to believe that I had ever viewed him as cold and unfeeling. My husband had more love for me in his pinky finger than most people would receive in their entire lives. There was no doubt in my mind that this marriage would last until the day one of us died. Cain would never let me leave, but more importantly, I would never have a reason to want to. I knew that he would give me the moon and the stars if I asked, even if it took every penny and the shirt off his back to do so.

When we arrived home, Cain carried me all the way from the front door to a room I'd never been in before. He opened it with ease, not setting me down until we crossed the threshold.

"What is this?" I asked.

"It's our room," he whispered. "I wanted something new for us, a space that you would be comfortable in. There's also a two-person jacuzzi in the connected bathroom, which I thought was a great addition. But of course, you can change anything you don't like."

I looked around the new bedroom I would share with my husband, amazed at the thought and detail he had put into it. It was clear that the space was designed to fit my taste rather than his. The walls were painted a soft cream color, and a giant diamond chandelier hung from the tall ceiling. There were two large windows on either side of the king-size four-poster bed, which was decorated with soft pink pillows and a white duvet. Along one wall were built-in bookshelves that reached all the way to the ceiling with a sliding ladder that would allow me to reach books at the very top. On the other side of the room was a huge vanity and cushioned chair that both looked as if they had been transported here from 19th-century France. The whole room reminded me of a Jane Austen novel. I couldn't have decorated it any better if I'd tried.

"Is it okay?" Cain whispered.

"It's perfect," I replied, giving him a bright smile.

He grinned, clearly pleased with his work. "Well then, Mrs. Kingston, your agonizing wait is over. I know you can just barely contain yourself."

He scooped me up in his arms, causing me to giggle. Ever so gently, he placed me down on the bed. As he looked down at me with love in his eyes, I knew my life was just beginning.

Epilogue

Brea

Four Years Later…

Finally, after years of planning and hard work, the New Leaf Preschool would be opening tomorrow. Cain stood beside me, his arm wrapped around my waist. After graduating, getting this place up and running had been my number one priority. And with my husband's help, it was now a reality. We had fifty students enrolled in five different classes and ten teachers ready to tackle the challenges of working with children who had troubles at home. Each child would spend two years learning with us before moving on to kindergarten. Hopefully, their time at New Leaf would give them a small jumpstart in their academic careers.

To my surprise, Evan and Enzo had decided they wanted to handle marketing and fundraising for the school. I was more than thrilled to have them involved. Mila, with her flair for design, had decorated all of the classrooms and was already looking at the possibility of opening a second location. It was all going exactly as

I had planned. Well, except for one thing.

Our little surprise, Caroline, would be arriving in just a few months. We had initially decided to wait a few more years before having children, but our baby girl had chosen to make her appearance earlier than expected. Although I was a bit shocked at first, Cain's confidence and relaxed attitude had washed my worries away. He would be the best father I could have possibly chosen for my child. No matter what happened, I knew he would protect and defend her with his life. That made me rest easy at night.

"I'm so proud of you, love," he whispered.

"I can barely believe it's real," I said. "I've been dreaming of this day for so long. Part of me never believed it would ever happen."

He motioned to the tall building decorated with colorful flowers and a big sign that said 'New Leaf' right above the giant front doors. "You did this, Brea. You made your dream a reality. No one should ever doubt your ability to accomplish anything you set your mind to."

I laughed softly. "Well, you paid for it."

He shook his head. "No, we did, love. What's mine is yours, remember?"

I placed a soft kiss on his cheek. "Well, if that's the case, then I think it's your turn to carry a watermelon-sized bump on your belly all day."

Cain chuckled. "I'll leave that to you. You're far

stronger than I could ever be. Don't you ever forget that. But if you do, I'll make sure to remind you."

I grabbed his face, pulling his lips down to meet mine. "You're the love of my life."

He wrapped his arms around me. "And you, Mrs. Kingston, are mine."

Abby Farnsworth is an award-winning Young Adult Paranormal Romance and Fantasy Author. Abby enjoys writing about a wide variety of characters within the Paranormal Romance and Fantasy genres, including faeries, vampires, witches, and werewolves. Her novels are all centered around romance, but also feature adventure and suspense. Her first novel, *EverGreen*, received the Literary Titan Silver Star Award, and her second and third novels, *Moonlit Skies* and *Fallen Snow*, received the Literary Titan Gold Star Award.

Abby currently resides in West Virginia and enjoys reading, nature, and long walks.

To learn more about Abby, her books, and current projects, take a look at the following:
#authorabbyfarnsworth
#theevergreentrilogy
Instagram: @abbyfarnsworth.writer
Facebook: @abbyfarnsworth.writer.poet

www.ingramcontent.com/pod-product-compliance
Lightning Source LLC
LaVergne TN
LVHW090609110826
845146LV00001B/312